HELL'S BOTTOM, COLORADO

LAURA PRITCHETT

MILKWEED
EDITIONS

The characters and events in this book are fictitious. Any similarity to real persons, living or dead, is coincidental and not intended by the author.

© 2001, Text by Laura Pritchett
(800) 520-6455 / www.milkweed.org / www.worldashome.org

Published 2001 by Milkweed Editions
Printed in Canada
Cover and interior design by Dale Cooney
Cover photograph by Karen Gordon Schulman
The text of this book is set in Granjon.
01 02 03 04 05   5 4 3 2 1
First Edition

Milkweed Editions, a nonprofit publisher, gratefully acknowledges the Star Tribune Foundation and the Jerome Foundation for providing special funding for this book. Milkweed also received support from the Elmer L. and Eleanor J. Andersen Foundation; Bush Foundation; Faegre and Benson Foundation; General Mills Foundation; Marshall Field's Project Imagine with support from the Target Foundation and Target Stores; McKnight Foundation; Minnesota State Arts Board through an appropriation by the Minnesota State Legislature and a grant from the National Endowment for the Arts; Norwest Foundation on behalf of Norwest Bank Minnesota; Lawrence and Elizabeth Ann O'Shaughnessy Charitable Income Trust in honor of Lawrence M. O'Shaughnessy; Oswald Family Foundation; Ritz Foundation on behalf of Mr. and Mrs. E. J. Phelps Jr.; John and Beverly Rollwagen Fund of the Minneapolis Foundation; St. Paul Companies, Inc.; U.S. Bancorp Foundation; and generous individuals.

Library of Congress Cataloging-in-Publication Data

Pritchett, Laura, 1971–
    Hell's bottom, Colorado / Laura Pritchett.— 1st ed.
    p.   cm.
    Contents: Hell's bottom — A fine white dust — Summer flood — An easy birth — Jailbird gone songbird — Dry roots — Grayblue day — Rattlesnake fire — A new name each day — The record keeper.
    ISBN 1-57131-036-3 (pbk.)
    1. Colorado—Social life and customs—Fiction.   2. Ranch life—Fiction.
I. Title

    PS3616.R58 H45 2001
    813'.6—dc21

                                                                  2001030966

                                                                        CIP

For James,
who adds to whatever he touches

CROSS FAMILY TREE

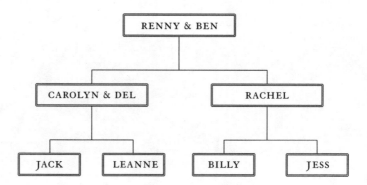

HELL'S BOTTOM, COLORADO

"Dry Roots" appeared in the June 1999 issue of *The Sun*.

The author would like to thank the following individuals for their advice, help, and encouragement: Lauren Myracle, Jack Martin, Rose Stehno Brinks, James S. Brinks, Judy Woodward, Lillie Fisher, Rita Rud, Tammy Minks, and most especially, James Pritchett.

HELL'S BOTTOM,
COLORADO

HELL'S BOTTOM

RENNY STANDS IN THE gravel driveway between the house and barn, her hands jammed into the pockets of a blood-splattered jacket. From there, she has a good view of the county road that runs parallel to the snow-covered foothills behind it, and she sees, at last, her husband's blue truck barreling down it toward the ranch.

The snow swirls around her in cyclones and drafts, crisscrossing in front of her eyes. She has to blink hard in order to see the outline of gray mountains, another ridge of foothills below, and the square blue block that contains Ben. When the truck takes the ranch's turnoff and heads toward her, she begins to take the pink plastic curlers from her hair. She tilts her head as she does so, and runs her fingers through the intended curls, through the segments of hair now wet with snow. She drops each curler into the pocket of her jacket before removing the next, all the time watching the truck approaching through the white flurry.

As Ben steps out of it, she wipes her dirty sleeve across her face before he can see her tears. "You're never around when I need you," she says as he approaches. "If I remember right, we're still running this place together."

He brushes past her, toward the barn. "Chains?"

"By the cow."

Sparrows gust out above their heads as they walk through the barn door. She watches Ben scan the shelves, his eyes adjusting to the dimness.

"Where's the plastic gloves?"

"Ran out."

"Damnit, Renny." But it is a quiet statement, more resignation than anger.

"Here," she says apologetically. She grabs a bottle of iodine from a shelf littered with cans full of horseshoe nails and screws, bottles of leaking ointments and medicines, piles of orange baling twine. She pours half the bottle over Ben's hands and arms, up to the elbow where he's rolled up his sleeves. He rubs the iodine in his hands like soap, tries to push the liquid under his fingernails before it seeps away and dribbles onto the cement floor. The iodine turns his hands a dull orange, the same color as her own.

This is the color, Renny thinks, of her daughter's fingernails the day she died. Rachel's nails were painted a burnt orange with drops of white polish on top of each nail to create a flower. The extravagance of those fingernails makes her crazy even now. The whole night makes her crazy. Stupid Rachel, peeling her truck into the driveway, running into the farmhouse, only to be followed, moments later, by Ray. Ben was the only one who had any sense. He got his shotgun, he pinned Ray. And Rachel, feeling safe, perhaps, or humiliated or furious or brave, had said, "You will never see me again. You will *never* have me." Which gave Ray just enough strength to break free, pull out his pistol, and shoot her. Shot by the husband she finally had sense to leave, Rachel was buried with small white flowers on her orange fingernails.

Ray has been sending letters of apology from the Cañon City Prison. Renny, for reasons she has not yet clarified with herself, posts these letters on the corkboard in the grocery store, alongside the notices for free barn cats and hay for sale. Maybe she hopes they serve as an invitation, one to everyone in town. To stop by and talk about this thing that is crushing her.

Even Ben would do, if he'd ever stop just to talk. She'd ask him in for coffee, and maybe she'd tell him what she's been meaning to. Ben, she would say, I know what everyone thinks. That we've been pulled apart, cut into pieces, and that I blame you. But I don't fault you for a thing. You can be slow to act and slow to stand up for anything, but not on that particular night. I saw you shoot above Ray's head to distract him, throw down the gun and tackle him. My God, how you tried. It would have been enough, had Rachel not spouted off. And this orneriness, this ability to fling out words was something I nurtured. Because Rachel was the only child like me. I wanted to see a part of me alive in someone else. Tough and mouthy and even a little mean. No, I don't blame you. I blame Ray. I blame the police, who took their sweet time in getting here. And a little part blames me.

Then, perhaps, he would hold her.

Ben strides out the barn's back door, which opens into the corral. "Tell me, please, that you've called Andrews."

"Hours ago, that idiot," Renny says, coming up behind him. Then, more quietly, "He may be avoiding me. I complained about the last bill so much."

Ben stops so he can look into her eyes and sighs quietly. She raises her eyebrows and shrugs, but he stares at her a moment longer. "Lord almighty, Renny," he says, turning away at last. "You damn well know better than to mess with the vet."

What he sees when he lets himself through the old wooden gate makes him wince. The cow is lying in the trampled, dirty snow, her belly towering into the air. A coarse rope halter crosses her nose but is tied to nothing, its end coiled near her face. The cow's breath rattles, a shaky *humpf* every time the air escapes her nostrils. Her eyes are blank and dark as she strains with a push. When she relaxes, she closes them—long, sweet eyelashes that make her look young despite her years.

"Hey, Mama," he mumbles as he reaches down and scratches the cow's ears, then runs his hand down her neck, over her bulging stomach, across her rump, down her legs. He wants her to know he's there, behind her, so that she's not surprised when he reaches inside her. He lifts her tail, hopes to see what he should—a tiny yellow hoof or two poking out. But there is nothing except for a small stream of blood. Kneeling in the snow, he slides his hand inside her.

He feels the plunge into warmth; tight muscles close around his forearm. His fingers reach out and touch the slick coat of the unborn calf, soft and warm, and his hand glides along the animal. Instead of a nose or a hoof, his fingers close around something slender, and he follows it down until he knows it's the tail. He yanks on it, hoping to get a response, but there is no movement.

He pushes in farther, until his arm is in past the elbow, going lower, deeper, feeling for a hoof. He's done it a hundred times before, turned a calf around inside a mother. But this calf is enormous; he cannot find a good hold, and when he does find a hind leg and pulls it, the calf doesn't move.

Ben pulls his arm out, away from the warmth. His wrist feels the sudden release from the cow's tight muscles, and his hand throbs as his blood resumes its normal flow.

As he steps back from the cow, he considers what hands are capable of. All they need is a little blood to flow through, and that's enough to pull a trigger, write a letter, post one up, take one down. He doesn't make special trips to the store, but each time he's there, he takes down the letters that Renny tacks up. He hates the feel of glances at his back, the attention his actions attract. But he's gotten used to smoothing over Renny's excesses, which is what removing these letters is all about.

He's got a stack of them now, crammed inside a notebook that's sitting in his truck. Ray writes that he's sorry, sorry because he really did love their daughter. It was a funny kind of love, he admits, funny because it made him crazy. He's sorry that the craziness is all the family thinks existed; more often than not, he writes, they held each other, made each other laugh. He assures them that good times did exist, and he describes them in detail. Rachel and her children shared their dreams with Ray and Ray shared his dreams with them, and they were nearly there, to the place where their dreams would have come together.

It all sounds, to Ben, like his own marriage in the early years. Enough energy came from Renny to make them both crazy. Each had hit the other, and it's a good thing, he thinks now, that he never thought of a gun.

He was about to break, one night, a night he just might have aimed the barrel and felt the trigger beneath his finger. Instead, his hands had curled up in fury. He managed to strike the kitchen table instead of his wife, and he managed to walk out of the house instead of toward her. That night he slept in a hotel. When he woke to the silence and rolled over in the clean sheets and regarded the simple room, he came to a conclusion: he would fight no more, even if it meant that in the end, he would lose.

He's not yet sure if he has. Now that he has moved away, the solitude and peace he encounters feel more like an upset, an unexpected win. Victory. But some gains are illusions, and he knows he might come tumbling down and find himself the loser. There are the nights, after all, that he misses her crazy banter, her misplaced energies. Though she could be cruel, her love was ferocious, and maybe he misses that most of all.

Renny and Ben are both staring at the cow, although they know that she won't offer a solution. The snow-flakes are huge and circling as they fall on her red hide. A crow squawks, and then there is near silence, quiet falling snow and the sounds of breathing. The cow shifts slightly, pushes, then sucks in breath and moans.

As if in answer, there's a crunching of tires on snow. Renny begins to pull out the remaining curlers from her hair as she listens to an engine idle and then stop. "Over here," she yells as soon as she's sure the vet has stepped from his truck. In a moment she sees Dr. Andrews trudge toward them, ducking his head against the snow. He is thin and tall; even the tan coveralls don't fill him out. As he climbs up and over the fence, his green eyes flick to Renny and he nods at her, then he looks at Ben.

"Thanks for coming," Ben says.

"About time," Renny says. "She's been in labor for God knows how long."

"Huge calf, turned backwards."

"It's dead." Renny jams her hands into her pockets. "Would have lived if you'd got here sooner."

"Cow's a tame one, Dr. Andrews," Ben says, as if to offer the only good news he can. "She's worn out. She won't give you any trouble."

"What a hell of a way to feed protein to the world." Renny raises her eyes skyward and shrugs, directing her confusion toward the heavens.

"All your cows are tame, Ben," Dr. Andrews says, slapping Ben's shoulder as he walks past him. "Get up, Mama." He picks up the rope halter and pulls. Ben pushes the cow's rump and Renny prods her gently with her boot. The cow rocks and then heaves herself up. Her head hangs down and she moans as she flicks her tail.

Andrews ties her up to a corral post and pulls on thin plastic gloves as he walks to the cow's rear end.

"Let's see what we have here," he mumbles, gliding his hand inside her. He closes his eyes and tilts his head toward the cow, as if listening for an answer.

Renny looks beyond him, to the rim of fields, an expanse of grass half covered with white. Bumps of yucca and sagebrush rise above the snow on the foothills that lie between their fields and the blue peaks beyond. Hell's Bottom Ranch. They bought it the year they were married. Fell in love with each other and with this section of land below the Front Range at the same time.

Ben used to joke that it was named for the place from whence Renny came. No, no, Renny would say, it's where I'm going. You better believe it, is what he'd say back. Their daughters learned this dialogue and would chime in, filling in one line or another. An old joke, but Renny liked to believe there was a little truth in it, too. She wanted to be the type of person who was a little hell swirled in with heaven. A little ornery to keep everyone on edge, intriguing enough to keep them around.

The truth is this: she and Ben had bought the ranch after the river flooded. Branches and debris were strewn everywhere along the bank. Walking along, they'd found a wallet, a cow's skull, a beat-up canoe, old fence posts, rusted barbed wire.

"Looks like the bottom of hell," she'd said to Ben, meaning that this land, protected with low foothills and a slow mountain river, was close to paradise.

"Hell's Bottom it is, then," he'd said. "Our heaven."

It's been a little of both. She's closer to hell now than she's ever been. A daughter dead, a calf that doesn't move, a husband who doesn't love her anymore. Heaven or hell? She rests her forehead on the cow's silky neck and repeats the question over and over. Either way, it's got her soul.

"Yep, dead," Andrews says, nodding to Ben. "We'll do a fetotomy, I guess. I'll need your help."

Ben watches Andrews head for his truck and then looks past him, toward the mountains, and thinks he might see, circling above the river, the bald eagle that's been hanging around. He wants to say something to Renny about it, and also about the young fox he saw yesterday and how it yapped at him—a strange sound, more of a raspy bleat than a bark. He'd like to tell her that he lets the dogs sleep with him on the bed, so that there's some weight and warmth beside him. He would like to ask her if she does the same thing, and if she responds with a yes, he'd like to make a joke about how the dogs' situation, at least, has improved since their separation. He clears his throat and faces Renny, who is staring in the direction of the river with some thought that has stilled her. She is blanketed in light snow, a dusting of white that has settled on her hair and jacket. She shakes herself and rubs at her nose with a hand he's sure is cold. She turns toward him, but looks past his eyes at Andrews, and so he, too, turns and faces the vet, who is returning from his truck with a black vinyl bag.

From it Andrews takes a long wire strung between two metal handles. Looping the wire in a circle in his palm, he closes his fingers over it, and pushes his fist, with the wire folded inside, into the cow. He rubs the cow's hind legs with his left hand as he works inside her with his right and hums a long conversation to her. "You'll feel better soon, mama mama mama sweet mama girl, bet you're hurting but it's almost over, sweet old mama."

Andrews brings his hand back out, holding the two handles. "I've got it looped around the hindquarter. You help me saw." He hands one handle to Ben. "Pull up and to the side, there."

"Sorry about this mama," says Ben. "You've been trying your hardest here."

As each man alternates pulling, there's a whir of the wire as it's pulled back and forth across the calf. The cow strains with this feeling of something moving inside her, and her ears flick backwards at this new sound coming from her rear end.

"I bet Danny Black has a calf you can graft on," Andrews says after a moment. "He just lost a cow."

"We'll give him a call." Ben uses his free hand to wipe the sweat forming on his forehead. He feels sick.

In all his years of ranching, he's only had to do this twice before, and each time it makes him want to quit the business altogether. He feels the tension of the line as it meets the bone of the unborn calf's leg, and he grits his teeth.

"Just about there," Andrews says. They saw for a moment longer and then Andrews indicates to stop. He reaches inside the cow and pulls. Ben steps back as the calf's hindquarter, severed from the groin to the point at the tail, slushes out in a waterfall of blood and thumps on the ground. The cow tries to turn, but the halter keeps her head in place, and Renny is there anyway, scratching her ears and blocking her view.

Renny has forced herself to watch, not to let her eyes wander even for a moment, not to let the wince inside her escape. Now she considers Andrews, watches as he closes his eyes and sticks the fetotome back inside the cow and feels for another place to fit the razor wire. His face is hard in a way she finds beautiful; his skin is tough and wrinkled, and gray stubble flecks his low cheeks and square chin. His forehead is wet, and a bead of sweat sinks down, causing his eyelids to blink rapidly over his green eyes.

She looks at Ben. His face is so familiar that she doesn't really see it at first. But she squints and concentrates. His hair is dotted with more white, she sees, and he's cut himself shaving just below the jawline. His eyes look soft and calm, as they usually do, calm despite the fact he hates what he's doing. She knows he's cringing inside, but even after all these years together, she can't see a sign of it anywhere.

"Just get through this, Mama," she says into the cow's ear as she scratches it. "I know just how you feel. Carolyn was easy. But that Rachel. I thought she was ripping me apart. The plight of mothers, I tell you."

It was Rachel, Renny recalls, who first suggested that Renny and Ben live apart. Carolyn agreed. Renny and Ben didn't have the momentum or cause enough for a divorce, their daughters counseled, but maybe, just maybe, they'd be happier apart. They began to devise plans, point out various spots where a new house could be built on the ranch. They admired various views. They talked about digging a well and running electric lines out, about the division of responsibilities. And all at once, last summer, it became real.

Ben called some old friends and disappeared with them to the back of the property, and soon a small log house stood at the end of the north forty. A few contractors, a little hassle, but surprisingly easy. Renny could have the old rambling house, Ben said, with its piles of junk, with the visitors driving into the front yard. What Ben wanted was some quiet, some remoteness.

The horses are back there now. She can barely see them huddled together, right in front of the small dark square that is her husband's home. The colt is trotting wildly around the group, throwing his head in the air. He suddenly bunches to a halt and kicks his hind legs up and out. She remembers what it's like to feel that way, the buzz of energy in her chest, in her throat. How she would shudder with the force of it, which was too much to control, her thoughts and laughter and love shooting off in every direction. She can recall the sensation perfectly. Her throat aches with its absence. Where once a joy swirled she feels a cavern, and though she does not know how to right herself, she is sure she has faltered, and how sorry she is for that. How incomplete she is now.

Ben decides to dump the pieces of this calf beyond his cabin, near the gully. He'll throw the head and hindquarters and body into the brush. The dogs won't dig through the mass of sticks to get to the calf; and besides, the body will be frozen to the ground soon, then covered by snow. By the time everything melts, the calf will have decayed. It's amazing, he thinks, how a life—laughter, arguments, little arms reaching out for him to carry her to bed—how everything ends up as clean bones. As far as he can tell, there's nothing more.

He looks up to find Renny watching him. Her head is tilted, her face soft—both of which are unusual enough to startle him. "I'm going to get Danny Black's calf," she says, lifting her chin, straightening out. "Before the snow starts to stick on the roads."

Ben nods and looks away. But once she's turned, he looks back up to watch her go, his eyes following the one pink curler she's left in the back of her hair.

"Would have been a bull calf," Andrews says as the other hind leg slips out of the cow and thuds down in the snow. "I bet a hundred pounder. She may be able to push the rest out. That big butt was the problem. Give us a push, Mama."

A waterfall of blood and yellow fluid comes with her strain. She relaxes and shifts her weight, then tenses. The rest of the calf slithers from her in a pool of membranes and blood and flops to the ground. A blue tongue hangs from the side of a small mouth, eyes open in a dead stare. Guts and the spinal cord protrude from the back part of the calf, and steam rises from them as blood seeps down and pools out into the snow. Immediately the cow tries to turn and thrashes wildly when she cannot break free of her halter.

"Whoa mama, good mama. You saved us a lot of work by pushing it out." Andrews gently tugs on the membranes hanging filmy-clear from the back of the cow. "I'll give her a few sulfur pellets for immediate infections and then give her a shot of penicillin. I'll leave a bottle and syringe. Keep her up here for a few days and watch her."

"I don't want to lose her," Ben says, running his hand down her rump. "She's a good mama."

"She looks like it," Andrews says from where he's kneeling, putting the coiled razor wire back into his bag.

"She would have protected this calf with her own life if she had the chance."

"Yes, I know." Andrews is standing now, ready to go.

"Leave the antibiotic in the barn, if you don't mind," Ben says, and then, winking, adds, "but if you want to get paid, you better leave the bill in my truck."

"Will do." Andrews smiles and then turns, with a wave, toward the barn.

Ben waits until he hears the truck start up before bending over to grab a piece of the calf in each hand. As he drags the parts toward a bench near the barn where he can sit and skin them, he considers how close this calf came to living—only a few degrees of circumstance. He's learned this much, how so much of life is the precarious moment, the sudden event, the surprise that spikes out of an ordinary day. How the rest—the bulk of life—is necessary to absorb these little bits. Absorb them and heal and wonder at.

They've been through the plains and the spikes of life together, Renny and he. It seems they're still circling and connecting where they can, to do what they must, on the ordinary days such as this.

By the time Ben is done skinning the pieces, Renny has returned with a sickly looking calf. She struggles under the weight of it as she carries it through the barn and into the corral. She kneels down in the snow and holds it against her as Ben rubs the hide over the calf's head. With orange baling twine, they tie the largest pieces of hide onto the shivering animal.

Once the cow is untied, she turns to sniff the calf, her nose running across the pieces of her own calf's skin. Then she moves to where the blood has soaked into the ground, and her nose hovers there, twitching. She considers the calf for a moment, sniffs it again, regards it suspiciously. It steps toward her and lets out a meek bawl. She moves forward then, slides her tongue over the calf's face and ears, and stands still as it teeters toward her bag of milk and sucks.

Renny and Ben smile, catch the other doing so, and turn toward each other, still smiling.

"At least," Renny says quietly, "we can still do that."

Ben nods, then holds out his hand toward the barn, an invitation for her to walk with him. They move together to the bench where the remains of the calf are piled, covered with a thin layer of snow. Ben picks up the trunk of the calf by the head and starts for the truck. Renny follows, a hind quarter in each hand. They throw the pieces of calf into the bed of the pickup, then turn to face each other.

"Wait," Ben says, though Renny hasn't moved. He wipes his bloody, orange-tinged hands on his jeans, inspects them, and reaches behind Renny. Gently, with the tips of his fingers, he takes the lone curler from her hair. She receives it with a good-natured scowl, starts to say something, then stops. He sees in her shrug what she intended him to, that she has no words that can begin to close this space. He nods his understanding and offers a sad smile in return. They turn, then, she toward the old farmhouse and he toward the truck, each ducking into the circling snow.

A FINE WHITE DUST

RAY'S HANDS SLIDE THE black, greasy rag along the barrel of his shotgun. That's what he reminds me of, grease. His face and hair and clothes are greasy, like he's been coated in a fine layer of oily dust. The only thing that doesn't look like Ray are the soft white feathers poking through the duct-tape patches on his red down vest. His dark eyes spot one, the same feather I'm looking at, which makes me think he can read my mind. He pinches the white down between his fingers and pulls it out. "Damnit," he says, squinting at it. "Let's go, Billy. Speed it up."

Billy's hurrying to put on his cracked tennis shoes, which are full of hay and caked with manure. His fingers look so thin, I can't believe that one day they'll be big like Ray's, that a body can grow until it reaches such a size. That my body will someday be as big as Mom's. I don't know how bones get long and skin stretches and fingers thicken, and sometimes I wish we could just stay small.

"Jess, you come too," Ray says, looking from the feather to me. "It'll be fun." I don't want to argue, so I pull on my old moon boots. Generally I only use them for chores, but they're faster to get on because they don't have laces and Ray, I guess, is not in the mood to wait.

Billy and I follow Ray out of the front-porch door and into the cold. I cross my arms to hold my jacket tight to my chest because the zipper doesn't work. Billy looks back at me and slows down until I have time to catch up, then winks at me as I jog along beside him.

There's a fine dusting of white that disappears when our feet touch it, leaving footprints of earth showing through the thin layer of snow. The sun should be close to setting behind the mountains but I can't see it because of the clouds, and having the sun covered makes the whole world seem cold and gray, but in a beautiful way, like everything is just a little silver.

We go through the back pasture and the wheat stubble, which the cows have been trampling, toward the empty irrigation canal. Billy helps me jump down. The canal is deep and narrow here, and frozen earth surrounds us on both sides, tiny ice crystals gleaming on the walls of dull brown. As we near the small pond, the canal gets flatter and wider, so we start crawling on our knees, then snaking along on our bellies. Ray points the gun ahead, holding it tight, moving with his elbows. Billy follows with his .20 gauge, and I'm last, clutching the cold earth close in order to stay low, because I don't want to be the one to spook the birds. Though I'd like to. But I'm not brave enough, so instead I concentrate on the mist clouds I make each time I breathe.

Ray raises his head, brings the gun up, slides his chapped finger to the trigger. Billy copies him, only his hand is smaller and browner and it's shaking. There's a long moment of quiet as they aim, quiet suddenly shattered, and I hold my hands to my ears as I jump up to watch.

The mallards take off from the calm water, honking and slanting up into the frozen sky. Ray moves like a crazy-fast machine: pump, aim, shoot, pump. Billy just has a double-barrel, though, and he only gets two shots off in the time Ray finishes seven.

But I'm mostly watching the ducks drop from sky into pond. Seven dark figures spinning down against a gray sky, spinning until they smack into the water. The rest escape fast, their scared, crazy noise growing dimmer as they fly toward the distant mountains, and I think, yes, that's where I would go too, toward those blue towering peaks where you can hide.

"Hot damn!" Ray says. "That was some good shooting."

"I thought the limit was three," Billy says.

"Yeah, the goddamn limit's three," Ray whines in a sissy voice. Then he says, "You go fetch those birds."

Which surprises me, but I guess I already knew that's how it happened before. Because once I walked into Billy's room and saw him sitting on the mattress on the floor, rubbing his small foot, which was gray-white instead of brown, and shaking so bad I thought he would crack apart.

I watch Billy unzip his jacket and pull off his shirt as he kicks off his shoes. He's facing away from me, looking at the floating ducks scattered across the lake.

"Won't he get cold?" I say it real soft, hoping maybe Ray won't even hear me.

But he turns and squints down into my eyes. "Not too much, honey. Though we should get a good hunting dog, shouldn't we? You talk Rachel into that, how about? Save your brother from having to go in there next time."

"Sure," I say. But he already knows I'd love to have a dog, a yellow Lab to be specific, because they've got that soft fur that's almost white. He also knows my mom will say no. No, because we're saving every cent so we can move, so we can get on with our lives. Move to our land, build a new house, and get ourselves together.

That's why Billy is wading out into that cold water. His shoulder blades jut out from his skinny back. I think Ray is staring at those little triangles under Billy's skin, too, and he says to me, but in a voice loud enough that Billy can hear, "Gonna make a man out of him yet.

Don't know who the father was, but he didn't leave Billy with much, now, did he?"

Billy hunches his shoulders and sucks in his breath as he steps into the water. When he's in as deep as his stomach, my eyes blur, so I just see the colors—his tiny skin-colored back in this big expanse of gray-blue. He starts swimming and I blink away the water in my eyes so I can watch him, watch his little head and revolving arms.

"Get the furthest one out," Ray hollers. "Then get the others."

Billy swims from one side of the pond to the other, and by the time he has all seven ducks, you can tell how heavy they must be, because he's struggling to tug their floating bodies to shore. Finally he stands there, dripping, handing the ducks to Ray. Ray starts whistling as he grabs them by their feet, holds up the bundle of birds, and eyes them up and down. I'm looking at the birds, too—at the wounds, how some are in the neck and some are in the chest, and how the blood makes its way down the glistening feathers and into the dark dead eyes. That's where it pools before dripping down.

When Billy's got his shirt and jacket and shoes back on, Ray hands us each two ducks to carry. Ray and Billy carry the birds in one hand, their guns in the other, but I hold one bird in each hand, away from me, thinking how sorry I am that they were alive a few minutes ago and now their blood is dripping at my feet. I want to get home fast, but the ducks are heavy with death, slick with water and blood, and they keep slipping from my hands and thudding on the thin layer of snow.

"Damnit," Ray says when I drop another one. "Billy, give me your shoelaces."

Billy bends down and pulls the laces out of his shoes and hands them up, and I'm thinking, I was stupid to wish my mom would meet someone, to think getting a dad would mean things would get better.

Ray says, "Now, I bet you two never had experiences like *this* before."

Blood from the birds soaks into the cotton laces as Ray ties them around all seven glistening necks. The other end he wraps around his hand. "Good memories," he says and starts walking again.

I'm thinking, poor Billy, those are his only shoes, the ones he'll wear to school on Monday. He gets enough teasing already, and when the laces dry they'll be brown with blood. But Billy's just jogging along like that's okay, shuffling his feet to keep the shoes on.

By the time we get home, it's pretty dark out and it's started to snow. Ray stays outside to clean the ducks. As we go inside, Billy starts to shake and he hugs himself like he's trying to hold his body together. Mom's sitting in the living room, leaning forward, piecing together a puzzle that shows an old log cabin in a field of flowers below some huge blue mountains. Her dark hair is pulled back into a ponytail and she looks so young, and I think maybe she's right when she says she had me and Billy before it was time to be a mom, and that really she'd rather be our sister. Her hand is outstretched, hovering over the puzzle pieces as she looks for the perfect one.

"You ought to hide those mallards, Mom. Only six allowed in a freezer at a time, and we got more than that just today," Billy says.

But she doesn't look up like he was hoping she'd do. Her eyes scan the pieces and she says, "Ah, no one's gonna come way out here and check. We don't need to worry."

So Billy bonks me on top of the head like he does sometimes, then goes into his room to take off his wet clothes. I sit down next to my mom and pretend to look for a piece she needs. As soon as she fits one and I see her smile, I touch her shoulder. "Billy had to go in the pond and get the birds. It's so cold out."

She's thinking about this, I can tell, gauging how cold it might be, gauging if it was a wrong thing for Ray to have Billy do or not.

"He had to swim with all seven ducks, and Mom, he needs a new pair of tennis shoes." All of a sudden, even though I don't mean to, I'm crying hard and leaning into her shoulder and I can feel her surprise, and I just keep gulping in air and the words keep coming out when there's air enough to form them. "His shoes are so old, and I need a new coat and it's so cold, and he shouldn't have to be swimming, he's not a dog." I'm just pouring out everything, but I manage to keep quiet about the main thing I'm thinking, which is, "How come you never notice any of this?"

Which is a good thing, because as long as I don't say it, she'll keep rocking me and holding me to her and saying "Yes, yes, you're right. You're all I've got" and kissing me on the head. I keep crying and it feels like I'll never be able to stop until I melt and dissolve into everything around me.

But then I hear the door shut and the crack and fizz of a beer being opened, and I lean against my mom and try to make it look like I'm just curled against her, taking a nap, and I try to even my breath and let the snot drip out my nose instead of sniffling it up, and I hold still. I can picture Ray leaning against the doorway with the beer in his hand, looking down at us. He says, "Ah, my two young, pretty ladies."

My mom is still deciding, I know. Is it worth it? After all, it's nothing too bad, nothing serious, just a swim in a cold pond. I feel her body relax under me, so I know she's made her decision, and I shudder when she does this, because I want to start crying again. I think she feels me because her body grows tense and now she's smiling up at Ray, probably cocking her head, trying to look pretty. She says, "Looks like Billy was wet and it sure is cold out. Isn't there any other way you could get those ducks?"

Ray's considering, deciding if he should get mad, because he thinks Billy is a wimp, and he probably thinks one of us complained, which I did, after all. He finally says, "Nope. No other way. I can't swim, as you know, because otherwise I would. Or we could get a dog."

She says, "Maybe we should, then," and I smile, because that means that we will. But I'm feeling a little sorry for that dog, because he probably doesn't want to swim in cold water, either. I'll love him so much, though. Enough to make up for everything else.

I decide that when Ray steps out of the doorway, I'll get off this couch and run to my brother. I'll tease him till he laughs, wash the blood from his shoelaces, have him look out his window at the falling snow. I'll love him so much it will make up for all the bad that comes his way. But I know, like my mom should know, that it won't ever be enough.

SUMMER FLOOD

LEX IS BACK IN town. This is why, no doubt, Carolyn has been dreaming of him, of his hands sliding into her jeans, insistent, pushing their bodies together.

These dreams are simply her way of working through her fears, her understanding that she is growing older. She knows this. She knows that she misses that falling-in-love love, the first time someone leans forward and oh, God, demands a kiss kind of love.

As she lies next to her husband, whom she really does love, she dreams of her old boyfriend reaching out for her. She is young and he is young, and the intensity that comes from youth and desire fills her pelvis and her heart. She wakes throbbing with the knowledge she is both in love and loved intensely. Then the pang of waking, of finding Del beside her. She is filled with an odd intense yearning, the kind of pain that refuses to dissipate, even now in the afternoon sun.

She's sitting in a lawn chair, watching the knife in

her hand as it slices through the white meat of an apple. These are the tart and bruised apples from the tree beside her, the ones with worms, the ones partly rotted. She refuses to let them waste. Instead she slices them, scatters the thin pieces across baking sheets, lets them dry in the sun. This winter she'll feed them to the horses as a treat. She promises herself this: in a few months, when she walks out to break the ice on the stock tank and greets the horses, she'll hold out a handful of withered apple slices in the palm of her gloved hand and remember this day and what it is to be warm, and remember this ache pulsing through her body.

She hopes that by then, the dreams will be gone, along with the heat of summer. The dreams are only a phase, after all, simple enough to dissect and understand. She stops to look up at the mountains and asks herself, quite gently, to quit these dreams. Then she grows a little angry and scolds herself for this self-made torment night after night, these visions that make no sense.

She picks up another apple from the pile beside her lawn chair and slices it into a big bowl that's balanced on her tanned knees. At the same time her son, Jack, and his girlfriend, Winnie, gallop up to the edge of the fence that separates the lawn from the field.

"Watch us," Jack shouts at her. He and Winnie look

flushed and bright from riding, and the horses are lathered slick with sweat.

"Go help your father," she says, pretending to ignore them.

"Ah," Jack says, waving her comment away with his hand. "Watch us first."

"Hey, Carolyn," says Winnie. "You're getting burnt."

"I know it," she says, looking down at her arms. They feel tight with the sunburn of yesterday, and today will only add to it. The heat is pouring down and seeping into her skin. She pulls her shirt away from her damp skin and holds it out, hoping for a breeze to waft in and touch her belly. The shirt is her daughter's black tank top, pulled from the laundry this morning. The day is too hot for a shirt, too hot for black. If the kids weren't around, she'd think about pulling the shirt off and working topless, and this makes her smile, the image of herself in this lawn chair, slicing apples, wearing no top.

"Are you watching?" Jack demands. "Are you going to watch?"

She stabs the knife into the apple and sets it on the wooden armrest of the lawn chair. "I'm watching," she says.

"Stand up so you can see better," he says.

She stands and shades her eyes with her hand. Jack, satisfied, leans toward Winnie and whispers something.

They turn the horses toward the pasture, pause, and then urge the animals into a gallop. Winnie and Jack ride side by side, hunkered down as they fly across the field. Suddenly, they arc away from one another, then towards each other, one horse passing just in front of the other as they cross. It makes Carolyn's heart leap, the two heading toward each other at such a speed. They do it again and again, galloping away from each other and then turning the horses toward one another, back and forth until they are stopped by the fence a half a mile away.

Carolyn rubs her hand across the middle of her chest and then raises it to wave as they turn their horses back around. They wave back before heading toward Del, whom she can barely see if she squints. He's fixing fence along the road that runs through their place. All day he'll be working—walking for miles, tightening the barbed wire here, replacing a strand there.

What she tells people when she speaks of her love for him is this: That she fell in love with him because he can fix fence and because he plays the piano. That she met him in a classical music class in college, that he tilts his head toward particular pieces of music, even if he's in a restaurant, even if he's in the old truck—that he does this and still knows how to break a horse, snap a chicken's neck, fix a fence. That when his hands rest on the piano keyboard, they are scraped, callused, dirty.

She loves that he will smile when Jack and Winnie

ride up and offer to help, knowing, as she does, they're happy enough to work just to be in each other's company, just to have the chance to recover quietly from the tumult that is rising within them. She remembers the sensation perfectly, and she's sure Del does, too.

She needs to see Lex for just a moment, she tells herself, and then the dreams will stop. In a flash, she'll see his failings, the reasons he was not the right one. That's why she sets down the apples and walks inside the rambling old farmhouse, through the porch with its collection of cowboy boots and work boots and muddy shoes, to her bedroom. In the mirror that hangs against the closet door, she considers the smudge of dirt on her cheek, probably from her work in the garden this morning. She leaves it there. She likes the look of it, the touch of care-free childishness it gives her face. There are wrinkles around her green eyes, though, the result of the Colorado sun. She runs her finger across the wrinkles and considers that some love is sturdy with deep roots, and some love is fresh and young, and that she should not kid herself about the truer of the two.

As she pulls out of the drive, she looks in the rearview mirror at her home, at the old white farmhouse with red trim. Next to it is the barn, shed, well house, chicken house—her little circle of red-and-white security. This is the life she wanted, and where she wanted to be, and so she should be at peace.

Twenty miles she's driving. She makes herself crazy. Despite her good judgment in leaving Lex and the others behind and marrying Del, she is driving twenty miles to drown a young and focused first love.

It's been a dry summer and the grasses have settled into a brittle, bleached green. The bushes that line the curving stream bed are darker, though—a fertile web zigzagging across the prairie. She turns off the air conditioner and unrolls the window. She wants the sound of the wind to fill the truck, to have the hot air whip itself away.

She drives through town, past the stores on Main Street, then flips a U-turn and drives by again. She pulls into the grocery store parking lot and considers her options. She could go home—this is what she ought to do. She could also drive ten miles more and visit Lex's parents' ranch, where he is no doubt staying, and think of some excuse for her presence.

Instead she just sits, listens to the country radio station and watches the cars on Main pass by. Nineteen years ago she moved back here with Del. Bought the ranch next to her parents' place, gave birth to Jack two years later, Leanne two years after that. She was too young to have married Del, probably, but he was the right one. Anyone who could play the "Moonlight Sonata" but wanted to herd cattle had to be the one.

She's thirty-nine now, though everyone is always surprised to learn this. She is tan, athletic, muscled. She is a bit more than good-looking; she knows it. Something about her youth, her looks, has filled her. Only recently has she felt an empty, hurt-filled space inside her. These dreams, of course, are her way of trying to fill back up.

Over the years, Carolyn has learned to trust her instincts. Things usually fall into place for her, as they do now, when she sees Lex's truck with his out-of-state license plates pull into the alley beside the cafe. He's with Al, an old friend and classmate who lives on a ranch near hers. They step out of the truck and head toward the cafe. Al blocks her view of Lex, but she can still glimpse his tall figure, his Wranglers and T-shirt, the way he rubs the back of his neck as he ducks his head and laughs about something.

She waits several moments before stepping out of the truck. She straightens her shoulders, lifts her chin, and walks quickly across Main, toward the cafe. Once in the door, she sees them sitting in a booth across from each other, each hanging on to the coffee cups resting on the table between them.

Lex has changed very little—still handsome, perhaps

even more so, with gray at his temples and creases around his brown eyes. There is an old scar across his temple, a fine white line that she used to trace with her finger when she nestled beside him.

She nods at Al, then turns to meet Lex's eyes. "I saw an out-of-state license plate and figured that was your truck," she says. "I just wanted to pop in and say hi."

Lex is thrown off guard; she can see that. They've been careful to avoid each other all these years. But he nods, moves over, and motions for her to sit beside him. She tries to shake off a shiver of nervousness as she slides in beside him.

There is a silence, a brief moment in which some sort of charge passes around the table. Then they are all talking, an effort to smooth over that charge, and she leans back and smiles. She hears about Al's horse that sliced its leg on a crazy contraption some idiot built for target practice on Al's land without Al's permission, a story she has already heard, and then listens to Lex talk about his place east of Des Moines. He's a farmer now, not a rancher, he says, and it's a hell of a lot easier to make money with soybeans and corn instead of cows. As he speaks, she watches him closely, as closely as she can without peering at him.

He says it's good to be back in town, and that it's not coffee they need, but a drink. They move toward the back, to the bar, and Lex orders a round. As he talks to the waitress, Carolyn's eyes meet Al's, and there is some sort of silent acknowledgment that this is an odd time of day to be drinking, odd but necessary, because this is indeed quite a situation to find themselves in. A drink, perhaps, will settle this buzz in the air and in their spines.

Carolyn drinks her beer and listens to Lex complain about the Midwest—reserved personalities, conservative religion, muggy air. But then, too, he says, it's not full of yuppies in spandex shorts, wanna-be cowboys, California snobs ruining it all. He speaks of genetically modified crops, and the fact that Europeans won't buy them, and the fact that Americans don't give a damn. How the grain elevators all have two sets of bins, one for the crops Americans will eat, one for shipping overseas. "Did you know," he asks, "that one Iowa farmer feeds 130 people?" He wonders where we got the idea, anyway, that America should ruin its soil feeding the world. "Every year America loses two billion tons of topsoil. Did you know," he asks her, "that we all stand on a thin layer of sustenance, we're just a few inches from desolation?"

She is surprised. She recalls leaving him for the fear that he would never see other choices, other possibilities than those immediately before him. Now she is living back at home, and he has moved on. But there was more to it, too, wasn't there? He lacked depth, empathy, the ability to hold inside himself the pain and joy of what is real. Or maybe it was just instinct, telling her to let him go.

She crosses her arms around her body. She's cold now—the air-conditioning has pulled the heat from her skin, and the sunburn makes her feel chilled. She wishes she could lean toward Lex and absorb some of his heat, either that or be out in the sun. It almost doesn't matter which—she just needs something, anything, to release her from the tight confines of cold.

They're on their third round before the past comes up. Al is laughing about a party they'd all gone to, one where everyone ended up drunk and naked and swimming in the irrigation canal.

Lex lets out a genuine laugh. He's agreeing with Al about how young they were then, how brave to go home to their parents, past curfew, dripping wet. But she knows that Lex is talking around the real thing. She feels what he does, the memory of the two of them, of his hands gliding along her thighs underwater, her wrapping her legs around his waist.

She looks up and his eyes are on her, serious and clear. Not only full of the memory but wondering, as she is, if there is more, a moment in the future in which they could curl their bodies around one another like that again.

She looks down at her beer and begins to pull the red label from the bottle. She's as buzzed now as she was back then. A rare occasion for her, but frequent enough in her lifetime to know that drunk is when she's most honest, that what she thinks and feels are then true. She is willing to believe that other people, when drunk, do things they do not intend. For her, though, the opposite is true. So she orders another beer, ready to get drunk enough to locate the deepest-dwelling spot of truth, and once she finds it she will look around to see what's there.

Lex notices the goosebumps on her arms and suggests that they go outside, and maybe, even, walk over to the high school. He steadies her as she stumbles a bit on their way out, and laughs with her when she laughs. She walks between Al and Lex down Main and toward the football field that borders the red brick building. She ducks her head and smiles, listening to them swap stories of old games and rivalries.

Out in the sun, her body melts into the warmth. She can again smell the flesh of apples mixed with the scent of her own salty sweat. She has always liked this salty smell—her summer skin, is what Del calls it.

Often, as it does now, the salty warmth makes her body ache. Summer and sex, Del has teased, are never far apart for his wife. Yesterday when she and Del found themselves alone in the cool farmhouse—he coming in from fixing fence, she wandering in with a basket of tomatoes from the garden—she'd pulled him toward the bedroom. They ran hands over damp backs and thighs and breathed in salt and the smells of outdoors in the cool, dark house.

She feels dizzy. The grass beneath her feet is cut short and she stares at it, hoping its preciseness will steady her. They are in the field, walking across the fifty-yard line, all three a bit wobbly and aware of the buzz that is not just inside them, but between Lex and Carolyn, and a little curious as to where it will lead.

Lex is telling them of a new invention made by the company he sometimes works for: pellets to put in the top of grain silos that kill bugs and mice as they sift down to the bottom. A good idea, that's what some farmer in Iowa thought, and he bought some. But when it rained, the rain seeped into his silo. There was a chemical reaction, a deadly gas was produced, and the gas drifted into the farmhouse. He tells them that the farmer's wife was sleeping on the bottom floor because she was nine months pregnant, and that she called 911 when she realized she was dying. Her family survived because they had been sleeping upstairs, survived because she warned them before she fell over dead. No one had tested the pellets for a reaction to water. "Can you believe it?" he asks, and then asks it again. He asks it with an inflection that means, all those scientists are jerks. And also with a smile, meaning, isn't life crazy and full of damn strange stories? Which it is, and she can see his point of view.

But she knows how Del would have told the story. He would have drifted off in the middle and turned his eyes away and possibly never finished it at all. His thoughts would not be on his audience, because he would be thinking of the woman and the unborn baby, of the possibilities that could never be.

The three of them are quiet, and she listens to the sound of their feet on grass. Al clears his throat, then, and says he needs to go back to the cafe, and there is an awkward moment as he tries to find a reason why. Then she is alone with Lex, and they turn back toward the cafe as well, but walk much slower. A silence drifts between them, one which she expects to be clumsy but is not. The tight nervousness in her body has given way to a warmer haze. She is very happy and so she closes her eyes, but still she cannot identify the source of the emotion.

"And how is your husband?" Lex asks at last.

"He's fixing fence today," she says. She tells him about her son and daughter, the dry summer, and their hay crop. The earth spins beneath her and her words are thick, and she tries to level out both, but mostly she is trying to clear up what she feels inside. The feeling is like trying to catch a handful of clear river water: she is only able to slow it for a moment in her hand. She feels enough, though, to know the water is good and that the river is Del. The truth of that comes charging at her, and the relief that comes with it causes her to let out a sudden laugh as she nearly loses her balance.

Lex steadies her and smiles. She agrees she's had one beer too many. But she is on the brink of tears. She is serious inside, trying to right herself and put the tumult back in order. As they near the center of the field again, she reaches out to take his hand. "Good-bye," she says, when he turns to face her. "It was good to see you."

He is taken off guard by this sudden farewell, but the look of surprise turns quickly into something else, and he holds her gaze with a question. She hopes her own look sends back something of the mornings when she dreams of what could be, of missing her youth, of the newness they once shared. But also of certain summer days, the ones that reveal all that is right. How fortunate she is to have found herself here, turning from him in the middle of a sunlit field, so sure of her direction.

AN EASY BIRTH

THE HORSE BUCKED AND sent Carolyn into a forward-flung arc, right into the edge of the creep feeder. She knew, in that instant in the air, that she was going to hit it hard. Arms out, eyes closed, face turned—all this her body did on its own. The only conscious response she had time for was to realize the extent of it, to think Jesus-God-this-is-going-to-be-bad.

She lies on her back in the snow. Turning her head, she opens her mouth so the blood will drain, then presses her lips together and tastes the salty tang. Her tongue feels the absence of a tooth in her lower jaw, and the gap startles her. Fear rushes up her spine and throat and pushes tears from her eyes.

Good God, she thinks, calm down. But as she thinks this, a stream of warmth spreads between her legs as her bladder empties, and again there is a surge of fear, though part of her is a bit surprised and embarrassed too. The sudden wet reminds her of the exercises she did years ago, during each pregnancy. She clenches her insides and holds her muscles tight, remembering.

This few moments after falling, the pain unfolds inside her. Craze-producing pain. She needs to thrash with it, but because she cannot the pain ricochets back and forth. She feels like she is giving birth to a child, the same sort of twisting back-and-forth confusion.

She vomits into the snow, feels her body throb as it brings up the contents of her stomach, and she's able to lift her neck just enough to let the fluid pulse out of her mouth away from her. As she does, she is dully aware of Fury in the far distance, heading for the river, kicking and rearing at the saddle, which has slipped under his belly. Blue is running after him, barking and running circles in the snow.

At least she is alone. She thinks this as she vomits again and then lies back down on her side and clutches at the snow, digging her fingernails into the hard-packed crust. Her children aren't young anymore, not wailing beside her. She's gotten them safely through childhood, and there's something to that.

She turns her face into the snow and bites at it, smashing her head down into the coolness, and as she does, she wraps her arms around her stomach like she did when she was pregnant. She can feel the precise source of pain now, not in her belly but in her leg and jaw and head, and soon it will subside, she is sure, and she will get up and somehow get home.

This morning, she had been summoned by her son to the vet clinic, where he helps out after school. Jack had called and said a mutt was in labor and that they needed an extra pair of hands. Carolyn arrived just in time to see a deformed puppy removed from the birth canal, where it had been stuck in the cervix.

"This one is causing all the trouble," Dr. Andrews had said. He held up a huge, bloated puppy. Its size was grotesque, especially the puffy head and the way the swelling deformed the nose and mouth. "Hydrocephalus, maybe." He turned and threw it in the trash can behind him.

Two more pups were in the uterus. Andrews brought one out from the mother, who was splayed out and strapped to the table. He cupped the pup in his palm while he tied the umbilical cord, and then handed it to Carolyn. She received it in her towel-draped hands and watched Jack take the other.

"Mine's not breathing," Jack said.

"Rub," Andrews said.

They rubbed the limp bodies under toweled fingers, looking down at the soft, sleek eyelids, tiny paws with soft pads, ribs showing through dark fur.

"Rub harder," Andrews commanded. "They're going to die." He stuck a needle into a glass jar and suctioned a brown liquid into the syringe. Then he took Jack's puppy, forced his finger into the small mouth, and gave the shot under the tongue. He moved so quickly, so fiercely, that Carolyn wanted to slap his hands and take the puppy away.

But she stayed still, and Andrews pressed his index finger against the puppy's chest and declared the presence of a heartbeat. He snatched Carolyn's puppy and gave it the same shot. Then he stuck a syringe up the tiny nose and suctioned out amniotic fluid. Cupping the puppy in his palms, he thrust it downward.

"To jar the fluid from the lungs," Andrews said. "Now do it. Then rub. Rub hard."

So with the puppy cupped in her palms, Carolyn flung her hands and the puppy down. All she could imagine was brain slamming against skull. But the puppy wheezed, drew in a wispy breath of air.

She can breathe, her heart is beating. She thinks of the basic human needs. Air. Water. Food. Shelter. In that order. "Ridiculous," she whispers out loud, feeling more blood trickle from her mouth as she does. You need a heart to beat and a brain to function. Those things she cannot control. She hopes her body knows how to function, to keep on doing its own thing.

The underbellies of gray clouds are puffing out huge, gorgeous snowflakes. She's watching them, trying to remember what the midwife said long ago about letting the pain pass through the body without resistance, when Blue's face appears above her, panting, his tongue dripping saliva onto her cheek. His tail is circling in huge arcs, and she wonders if he's dumb enough to think she's playing. Surely he must know something is wrong. She pushes him away with her right hand and closes her eyes. Pretend you are a wet noodle sinking into warm water, the midwife had said as she and Del lowered Carolyn into a bathtub. I am not a goddamn noodle, I am a goddamn lobster thrown in live, she hissed at her husband when they were alone. He had laughed, as she hoped he would. How strange, she thought then, that the human mind can still hope for a sense of humor, even when being both ravaged and dulled by the throes of pain.

Blue is sniffing her crotch, at the wetness between her legs that has now turned cold. If he lifts his leg on me, she thinks, I swear to God I'll kill him. But he only paws at her, his nails clawing into her side. She winces and tries to roll away. He slides his head under her hand, wanting a pet. Good God, she thinks. Even now something is being asked of me.

She's given and given. Given to each child and, for the most part, gladly. Giving hasn't made her bitter or sad. She hasn't been drained. Jack and Leanne—she has been granted these two children. They're sturdy souls now, but there was a time when she waited for them to slip away from her, too, as her other babies had, the three miscarriages in early pregnancy. She was unsure of their essence, each time, until she held them wet and screaming in her arms. They'd lived such precarious lives inside her, she felt they deserved sanctuary in the world—she'd begged with the forces of nature to protect them, to lash out at her if need be, but to insulate them. And they do seem strong. Her Extra Hearty Varieties she calls them. They're like winter wheat stressed by drought, which turns out stronger in the end, stronger and with deeper roots.

Jack, in his last winter at home, seems to be turning cold. "I need out of here," he accuses. Meaning, Carolyn knows, too many rules, restrictions, too much of a mother's love. She understands, and still she feels betrayed.

She was determined, when she drove to the clinic this morning, to find a connection, reestablish a bond. She's felt recently that the pain of her son leaving her this time was too much to bear.

The horse, she decides, will run to its pasture near the house. The kids will be home from school and Del is around doing chores. One of them will see the horse and investigate. Once she has recovered, she will tell them that she'd been checking to see if the calves had eaten the grain in the creep feeder. She'd been looking at the salt block, at how the cows' tongues sculpted it, and have they ever noticed that, how smooth and hilly a salt block becomes? A bird had whooshed out of the grass, right next to the creep feeder, making Fury buck. The bird flew up as she flew down, and she felt its wing graze her hair.

She reaches out to touch the air above her. The snow-flakes have become smaller and the wind is picking up. She is so thirsty. She opens her mouth to the snowflakes and feels the air turn her mouth a sharp cold.

This morning she was too hot, and she'd complained about the temperature at the clinic. Stupid Andrews, flinging those pups around. The limp puppies couldn't bear such fierce energy, Carolyn felt sure. Saving re-quires softness. The pups had lived, though—opened their tiny mouths in noiseless mewls, stretched their necks sideways, searched for their mother's teat.

"There's nothing like nursing," Carolyn used to tell people, "to make you feel like a mammal." After nursing Jack, she never regarded female animals without the knowledge that she and they were not so different. She could imagine mama dogs feeling puppies rolling around inside them for the sixty-some days of gestation. Cows must feel a calf's strong hooves during those nine months, just like a human. She's relieved to know she can remember these details. She's relieved she has the memory of pulling a few calves herself, on afternoons just like this, cold and snowy. She's relieved to know that her body could support a baby after all, that she has two, that she can remember their names. Her brain has not been thrown forward into skull.

She is panicking, though. She can feel the surge of fear rising up through her body, her heart constricting. How, she wonders, does that happen? The heart is only a muscle. Yet it can open and close and tighten and relax, not like a muscle but like a sensation. After all, some hearts are strong and some are weak, and it has nothing to do with strength of muscle.

"Shackleton." She says the name out loud. Then a bark of laughter escapes her. Finally she is able to use this bit of information! If ever caught in a perilous situation, she used to think, she would remember Shackleton's expedition. His tenacity would guide her. She's delighted she remembered, delighted to be delighted by such an absurd thing at a moment like this.

"They were in Antarctica, and they shot their dogs, you know. Just so the dogs wouldn't suffer and starve." She whispers this to Blue, who is lying next to her, panting. She looks him in the eye. "Blue, how about you run home and get some help?" He cocks his head and leans forward to lick her cheek. "Go home," she commands. He rolls onto his back and wiggles in the snow.

Survival stories. Here's her chance to do what she'd imagined in a situation such as this. She searches her memory for brave and tenacious hearts. *Into Thin Air. The Perfect Storm.* Donner party. Ah, yes, that one about the two enemies trapped beneath a fallen tree. Stuck there just long enough to talk all their differences out. One can see, but the other has been blinded. They hear a noise, they rejoice—someone has come to save them! The one who can see lifts his head to look, a smile upon his face. Only it's not rescuers but a snarling pack of wolves.

You idiot, she thinks. That's not a survival story, that's a death story. What a way to go, torn apart by wolves. There's a mountain lion out here; she's seen its tracks. "I'm not going to be eaten by a mountain lion," she whispers, rolling her eyes at the clouds. But this thought has given her the impetus, finally, to sit up. Because the snow beneath her is tipping and spinning, she squints at Blue until the sickness created by the revolving world subsides. He has leapt up and his tail is circling furiously. "Remember," she tells him, "how you always peed in the kitchen?" It must be an unnatural sensation, this holding of urine. She keeps her eyes on the snowflakes on Blue's nose, watches as they melt and turn to beads of water.

She sees, when she is able to take her eyes from him, quite a lot of blood on the snow, which is packed down from cows' hooves. Various crevices are filled with blood, a spiderweb of red soaked into dirty white.

She takes the glove from her hand and presses it to her head, wanting to feel the sticky warmth she is sure is there. Her earlobe is cut, only partly attached to her head, in fact. But it is her jaw that sears with pain. Her brain seems fine, though. The first question she asked her children any time they'd been injured was, how's your head? Protection of the essential.

She imagines how she will be when she wakes tomorrow, safe in her bed. She will be frowsy-headed instead of taut, warm instead of cold. No whipping flurry. She rests her head in her arms and listens to her breathing. Hers will be soft, a very soft saving.

Once the puppies were saved, Andrews had turned his attention to the mother dog, who had been drugged and strapped to the padded table. Her respiratory monitor beeped and the rubber bag inflated with each breath, which was, she remembers being told, thirty times per minute. Andrews told her this as he stood above the mutt, sewing the layers shut. First the uterus. Then the muscles, then the tissue between muscle and skin, then the skin. Twelve-pound clear nylon, made dried-blood brown with Betadine.

As he worked, Andrews also explained about the surgical light overhead. It was made, he said, with special mirrors to prevent the shadows of his hand from being cast into the body, so he could see. Also, this light cast no heat, so his hands wouldn't get hot. No shadows, no warmth. How strange it seemed to her that a light could be voided of its basic properties.

She's sobbing now. She can't help it, can't stay calm. Blue nudges her with his nose, whimpering. He licks the blood at her neck, and she can smell it too, the metallic salt of it, and the scent of vomit mixed with vanilla-smelling traces of shampoo in her hair. The wind is howling, blowing snow from the ground into her face. She twists so that she faces east, away from the wind and toward the direction of her house.

Come on, she commands herself. Pull it together. She's suffered and been fine before. Years ago when she curled up in bed and felt her body cramp and expel the beginnings of a baby—what had she done, then, to comfort herself? As she miscarried the babies, one before Jack and two before Leanne? She can't remember. She only remembers whispering, each time, "Good-bye, baby. I would have loved you."

They moved the mutt to a blanket on the floor, and as Andrews wiped down the operating table and Jack loaded the washing machine with bloody towels, Carolyn stroked the dog's ears as she came out of the anesthetic. Jack placed the two pups against their mother and they immediately nudged against her and suckled.

Jack stood beside Carolyn and watched. He would blush and move away if she told him he once nursed in a similar way, lying in the bed next to her, his face pressed against her breast. So she did not tell him of the tenderness that seized her, for his grown-up self beside her, for that baby he once was.

"You grew up with such speed," she decides she'll tell him one day. "Suddenly a spark of ornery attitude, with a girlfriend, keeping a quiet sad distance. The day I helped with the pups, the day I got bucked off Fury, remember? As I lay in the snow, I decided I was grateful that all that was even possible."

Something inside her feels like cracking. Her heart and head and uterus turned out good, but she knows she'd better do something soon. She cannot walk. She does not know what is wrong with her leg but knows from the pain that it will not support her. She begins to crawl, pulling herself toward the farmhouse. Blue is beside her, wagging his tail. "Shackleton Shackleton Shakelton," she says. It's been a long time since she cried from pure physical pain; she had forgotten how much a body can suffer.

As long as she doesn't look up and acknowledge how

far she has to go, she is sure she can continue. She will crawl across the field, down the lane, alongside the barbed wire fence to home. She will do it by force of will, she decides, just as she willed her children into being.

She's startled when Blue barks, and she raises her eyes long enough to watch him bound toward a figure coming up the lane. Someone on Fury. She catches sight of Jack's black cowboy hat dusted in white. He has seen her, has urged the horse into a gallop. She waits until she hears him call "Mom Mom Mom" before she sinks down. Then she closes her eyes to better hear the approach of hooves on snow, so she can focus on how it feels to have her son rush to her body.

JAILBIRD GONE SONGBIRD

HE'S NOT DANGEROUS, SHE says. It was just a drug bust
and he doesn't have a mean bone in his body. Further-
more, it was just some marijuana growing by the side of
the road, for God's sake, and don't our law enforcement
officers have anything better to do with their time? Now
he's out and has to make a new life on his own, and I
ought to try to be a little friendly instead of avoiding him
all the time. According to her, I'm being very closed-
minded and judgmental.

"Grandma Renny," I told her, "you're always bring-
ing weirdos here. But this tops them all."

"Leanne," she said back, in the same whiny tone I
had used, "when you grow up, you can live your own
boring life full of safety and no surprises. Just like your
mother. Carolyn's always been like that."

Well, she just doesn't see what I see, which doesn't
surprise me all that much, because she can be naive.
Slade clearly is just not right in the head, and you never

know what someone like that might do. For one thing, he has these blue eyes, so blue that they just don't look right on a human—eyes that were meant for a dog or a cat or a wolf. But it's not just that, it's also the crazy look he has in those eyes. A wild kind of look, all intense, like he's all wired up. Plus there's his name, of course, which just doesn't sound right. All this surface stuff adds up to something big underneath, I can tell.

Just wait till he rapes me. Then she'll be sorry.

But even my grandfather, Ben, is getting to like him; I can see that. Says he's a good worker. Slade has already cleaned out the barn, fixed the tractor, and helped pick up hay. Today they're out building a new fence around the bull pen. I can hear Slade whistling as I walk down the lane to check on their progress, and I have to admit, it's a pretty good whistle. It's that "Delta Dawn" song, which probably makes Ben as happy as anything, since that's his favorite song for road trips, which is always causing me to smile, because poor Ben doesn't know how dorky it is to sing old songs when you're driving along, especially when Renny chimes in. That kind of thing just cracks me up. But by the time I get closer, Slade has switched to that famous Mozart song, which we happen to be practicing in band, and which happens to be one of my favorites.

He's using the fence stretchers to pull the barbed wire tight as Ben hammers in the U-staple to the corner post, and I wonder if that barbed wire reminds him of the fence around a prison. I wonder if he ever tried to escape. When we get back to the house and we're alone in the front yard, I take off my glasses and pretend I'm looking at them for dirt and dust, so that I don't have to look at him, and I ask him.

"Slade, you ever escaped before?"

"Nope," he says. "I served my time. I'm a jailbird gone songbird."

"What's that supposed to mean?"

He says, "I'll tell you a story."

Already I'm impatient. I don't want to hear a story. But he starts up anyway, so I put on my glasses, flop down on the picnic table across from him, and stretch out my legs so I can get a tan.

"I had this picture of my wife, see, in this locker in the jail."

"You had a wife? You had lockers?"

"Well, I had a wife, and we each had a locker in the dormitory."

"What happened to your wife? Where is she?"

He waves his arm at me, showing that no more questions are allowed, and then goes right on. "I had a locker, and this gang of mean guys kept breaking in and stealing that photo of my wife. When I'd get a package or some cigarettes, I'd have to pay them to get my own picture back. So I'd give them my cigarettes and a chocolate bar, get my photo, and next week, they'd steal it again."

"Why didn't you hide the picture? Or carry it around with you?"

"Because I had a plan." He stops to scratch his jaw and then glances around the yard and leans real close to me. "This is confidential, by the way."

I give him the thumbs-up. But I'm thinking, what a moron. His story probably isn't worth repeating anyway.

"I said to those fellows, I said, 'You better cut it out, I'm telling you, or something bad is coming your way.' I wanted to give them fair warning, see. But they didn't pay no attention."

Suddenly a doubtful look crosses his face. "Naw, I guess I shouldn't be telling you this story. For one, you're too young. And for two, you'll tell your grandparents, and I don't want them thinking bad about me. I like it here. And you have to understand, it was in a certain situation . . ."

He makes me plead a little and promise silence, and he keeps postponing telling me, and here I am begging to hear a story that I never wanted to hear anyway. Finally, he starts up again. "I got the mercury from the inside of a thermostat that was on the wall in the gym. You know mercury? That's a chemical that—"

"I know what mercury is," I say.

"Well, I sweated open a pack of cigarettes, and put

the mercury on them. Then I got a candy bar that my wife had sent me. Which was a Milky Way, which is what I asked for, which she thought was strange, because I don't like Milky Ways. But they got that puffy stuff in the middle, right?"

"Right," I say when he pauses. "I know about Milky Ways."

"I bit into it so that the foamy chocolate stuff was showing, and I put the powder from a fluorescent light into the candy bar. You just break a light, see, and you scrape the powder out of it. Then I folded the wrapper down and left that candy bar in my locker. I washed my hands clean. Like that guy in the Bible. Pontius Pilate. I didn't make the decision, I just provided the opportunity. Because it was in my locker. And if they took it upon themselves to steal it and eat it, then they got what they deserved. I figure God can't get mad at me for just sticking mercury on some cigarettes. I had no malice. I wasn't offering them a smoke or a candy bar. They took it. They got themselves in trouble."

"Well, what happened?"

"They broke into my locker. They stole my photo, and they stole the cigarettes and the candy bar, even though it was half-eaten, which goes to show their state of mind."

"And?"

"And they all got sent to the hospital. The ones who

smoked the cigarettes lost their teeth and hair and fingertips. The one who ate the candy bar had to have a goat stomach put in. That's what the doctors did, believe it or not, put in a goat stomach."

"You nearly killed them!"

He just shrugs at this and gives me an innocent look. "A week later, the warden calls me in. He says, 'If they would've died, Slade, I would file murder charges against you.' But they didn't die, they just got transferred away. Which is what he wanted, because they were mean. But, after all, I hadn't done anything except leave a candy bar in my locker. I'd done that warden a service, and he knew it, too. I started getting a break."

Ben walks out of the house right then with a glass of lemonade for me and two beers for Slade and him, which is a relief, because I don't know what to say to Slade about this story of his. When Ben puts the drinks down, I slug him in the arm, and he pretends to box me back.

"I was just telling Slade here," I say to him, dodging his fists, "how much you like 'Delta Dawn.'" I roll my eyes and slug him in the belly, and Ben laughs and says something about me not knowing what good music is, and he starts getting serious about this fake boxing, tapping me with his fast hands, just a faint tap with his fingers instead of a full-force hit, showing me I'm not a good blocker, not very fast, and he's so good it makes me laugh. Slade laughs too, and then bursts into a whistle of that song from *Rocky*. After a while Ben eases up on me and lets me punch him in the arm, so I get the last hit in, and then we just sit around the picnic table. The sun's setting over the Rocky Mountains, and there's a meadowlark singing, and it's getting cool and quiet. Slade starts whistling softly, some tune that's soft and low, something I've never heard before.

We stay like that for a long time until Slade laughs. He nods at the horses, who are trotting through an open gate into the lawn, heading right for the garden and apple tree. This is no surprise, since it happens every day. Stoney has learned to open the latch with his nose, and no one has gotten around to putting a better latch on the gate yet. I don't think anyone will, either, since it seems to be some kind of ritual, this letting the horses get out and then chasing them back in.

We all get up and start walking toward the horses, and Slade starts whistling "Desperado." When we split up to circle them, I stay close to Slade, because I've got a sneaking suspicion, just from instinct, and I need to know the answer.

"So this . . . mercury thing," I say. "All that happened when you were in the county jail for a drug bust?"

"Oh, no," he says. "That was when I was in prison in Texas."

A-*ha,* I'm thinking. There you have it. I've got an

instinct that other people don't. Renny and Ben don't know the half of it. This guy is crazy. I look at him waving his arms at the colt, and I say, "What were you in for?"

"Sinking boats. See, you steal a boat that's in the harbor and take it to a real private spot that's not too deep and you sink it. You recover it later, after the whole thing's blown over, and the original owner has gotten his insurance money. Which is good for him, I figure, because he gets a new boat. I get a boat. And the only one who gets screwed is the insurance company, and they deserve it."

"Yeah, right. What'd they do to you?"

"They dump sick people off their medical insurance, for one. They cheat all their paying customers. They're the biggest criminals around. So I don't mind playing a little Robin Hood."

I snort, because that's rationalization for you. I myself am an expert at it, so I can see it when it's coming. I scratch Stoney on the neck and then grab his mane to guide him through the gate, and Slade's got the colt around the neck, but he's having a harder time of it, since that colt doesn't quite have the procedure down.

"I got thrown in prison," Slade says, after the colt calms down. "And right away, this guy starts giving me a hard time and I took exception and we had it out. Then they put me in confinement because they thought I was a violent person. They tell you, if you don't fight, then good, but if you don't fight, you die, so what good is being good? Then they send me to the worst prison in Texas because I'm a Yankee, because I don't have a stupid Texas drawl and ask for"—and here he raises his voice and says in a Texas accent—"some corn frittaaaas an' friiiiied chicken." He smiles and opens his crazy eyes wide. "They sent me to Bloody Ham, the worst goddamn prison in the world." Then he goes and changes the subject on me. "Did I ever tell you that I'm carrying the torch for Celine Dion? That Gloria Estefan, too. My God, they have voices. There's something about music that reminds me of all the good."

He starts humming and shaking his head as he hums, and I know he's hearing the whole song in his head, every piano key and tilt of the voice, because that's just how I hear songs too. Even though my pitiful self can only produce a wavery off-tune hum, I still got the thing going perfect in my head. Usually, my brain's got everything about right, and I can trust whatever's going on up there. But this time, I don't know. This guy is more wily than I originally thought, and something about him makes me shiver. But he's humming away with his eyes closed and he looks like he's quiet inside, quiet and peaceful.

"Leanne." Slade opens his eyes and stares at me over the colt's back. "You know, there's only one excuse for killing a person. If they're trying to harm you or someone you love. I wouldn't ever do anything to hurt you or your family."

I'm a little embarrassed at that, because it's too close to the truth, and I hate for someone to see through me. "Give me a break," I say. "Did Renny mention something? Because she thinks I'm a little scared of you, but I'm not."

"She didn't say anything. I can just see it."

"No way, Slade. You don't scare me."

"There I was in the county jail," he says, "after I thought I had my life turned around. And I really had, except for an occasional smoke of dope. There I was back again, and I was feeling real bad, and I thought the devil had me by the butt and was dragging me down again. I said, 'Boy, do I need an angel of mercy.' Just then, your grandmother walked in. Renny visited me, because, as you know, we were friends when we were kids. She offered to let me come and stay, and I'm telling you, it's more than anyone else would have done, and I won't ever forget that."

We've got the horses at the gate and lead them through. They shake their heads, grumpy to be back, but I don't see what they're complaining about, since they've got a huge pasture full of green, and everyone says these horses are the most spoiled animals around.

We lean against the fence and wait for Ben, who's coming with the two bay mares.

"My wife just didn't want to wait while I was in prison," Slade says all of a sudden. "I don't blame her. She left long ago, and I haven't had a lady friend like her since," he says and winks. "Although I'm thinking of writing that Celine Dion. You think she'll write me back?"

He's asking it so serious, like maybe it's even a real question, like maybe he even has a chance, that I have to laugh. "No. She's not going to write you back."

"Well, then," he says, looking all disappointed. "Even a regular old friend would be nice." He raises his bushy eyebrows while looking right at me, and those eyes are so clear blue they make me squint. I force myself to look right at them, but I just don't know what they're telling me.

I flip Stoney's mane through my fingers and turn to watch Ben, who's coming our way singing "Delta Dawn." Mozart's playing in my mind, and Slade's whistling something new again. So I reach out to slug him in the shoulder and say, "I guess you're just a jailbird gone songbird." But just in case, I think, I'll keep watching those eyes.

DRY ROOTS

THE WHEAT IS STARTING to turn, flashes of deep gold streaking through tall, waving green. Before we moved to Colorado, I used to think wheat grew golden yellow, like those photos you see in calendars. I suspect most city folk think that. They don't realize that wheat grows up green and living and then it dies, and that's when it becomes useful.

This wheat will be harvested next month. Dry weather is good now because there can be only 15 percent moisture in wheat when it's harvested. Not every girl knows that. But I'm learning everything because this time, Mom says, we're staying.

Billy's not looking at the wheat, though. He's staring straight ahead, arm hanging on the steering wheel, trying to look cool. His face is still red, but the slap mark doesn't show white anymore; it's just disappeared into the rest of his cheek. There's a wet line running down his face, but it looks like it's drying fast. He's driving slower now and so it's just like he says—if you wait, things will always get better.

And this is true, because Billy says in a happy voice, "Well. He sure scared us this time, didn't he?"

"Yeah." My voice sounds too quiet, so I say it again, louder. "Yeah! He sure did."

"Ray's just having a bad day." Billy nods, agreeing with himself.

But then a new tear starts and I know he doesn't want me looking at him, so I stare at the old .22 rifle that's resting in the seat between us. Billy was trying to teach me how to shoot it last week. I didn't get very close to any prairie dogs, but we laughed hard then and that makes me smile. We're on County Road 14L and up ahead is Baxter's windmill and water tank and cows. The wind is rushing in through the windows and we're almost to our land, a quarter-section, 160 acres.

Sometimes I think if they lose this land I might die. I don't even take the quarters and dimes off the dryer anymore because maybe they'll need them to help with the payments. I just let the money sit because I want to move up to this land and build a house, just like they say we will. I want to live on this prairie that stretches and stretches, just like how my heart feels when I think of it, expanding so far into nowhere that nothing can stop it, not even the soft gray mountains I see in the distance.

Billy parks the truck, and there it is, our land.

Spreading before us, pale and bumpy, rolling and curving its way to the horizon. Someday our house will break up the view, someday our house will be in the middle of our trees—a windbreak of Rocky Mountain juniper. They're still only about two feet tall, and they grow slow, but they're the best drought-resistant trees and that's what you need in a place like this. One hundred in each row; four rows making up a windbreak. It took forever to plant them all. We spent most of last summer doing it—marking off rows, digging holes, putting in those pellets that hold moisture, and planting each little tree. And then we hauled water out here every weekend to help get them started. Each time I poured water around their roots, I'd think that they were smiling and lifting up their little needles to hug me. A 60 percent survival rate is a good one, and Ray says we shouldn't hope for more. But they're all looking good right now, if you ask me, and I just can't wait. They're going to surround us someday. Surround and protect us.

I jump out of the truck, walk over to the closest tree, and bend down and feel the needles. The new growth is soft and green against the dark, brittle needles, so young and alive next to all this sagebrush and yucca and prickly pear cactus. I hear a faraway meadowlark and the wind, and I stand up and stretch and stare at the pale land and turquoise sky.

From the truck Billy calls, "Hey Jess, what's that?"

My eyes follow the direction of his arm. There in the far distance, all by itself, is a rust-colored animal. It could be a cow, except it's standing all wrong. Its shoulders are high, and its butt is down low.

"Looks like a baby buffalo," I call back.

Billy climbs out with the rifle. "Let's go check it out," he says and takes off running.

I have to move fast to keep up, running way past our trees and scrambling through the barbed-wire fence that separates our land from old man Baxter's. He'd be mad if he knew we were on his land because he's an ornery old grump, liable, I hear, to shoot just about any-one. That thing up ahead must be one of his calves. I can see now that it's reddish brown with a white face, like the Hereford cows grazing out here, but the shape is all wrong.

"Billy!" I yell. "I know what it is!"

He stops running and looks back at me.

"It's one of them cows that's been mutilated by a UFO!"

I see his eyes grow big for an instant, but then he says, "Nah. You read too many of them space books. I bet it's a calf with a leg stuck in a prairie dog hole." He waves me forward. "Come on!"

He's running on ahead and I don't want to just be standing there where a rattler might get me, so I start running again. I'm watching the ground for snakes and not looking up, and I almost run into Billy. As I stop where he has, I hear the bawling of a calf.

I look up and step behind Billy because I want to hide behind him. He's shaking his head and whispering "Oh, Jesus, oh damn" over and over.

The calf has no legs below the back knees. No little hooves, no thin ankle. In front it looks like a regular calf, long eyelashes, dirty white face, soft pink nose. But the spine curves down because the back legs aren't the right height, and all it has is two round stumps for back legs, covered in a dark dried blood.

The calf bawls again and then takes a step away from us with the two front legs, limping and dragging the bloody hind legs behind.

"Holy oh my God," Billy whispers.

I back up and try to pull him with me. "Billy?"

He jerks his arm free from mine. "They're both cut off. I don't know why. Maybe the back legs froze when it was born this winter and Baxter chopped them off at the knee."

"Nobody'd do that, Billy."

"Yes, he would."

"No."

"I've heard of it. I bet Baxter's just hoping this calf lives awhile and gains some weight. Then he'll make some money when he sells it for butcher. Look, you can tell the wounds are old. There's some hide grown over the stumps. But the hide keeps ripping away because it's gotta walk on its knees. I bet it's three months old." Billy bends down and looks beneath her. "It's a little heifer."

"A girl?" Even though I don't want to, I'm crying pretty hard. "But why'd he do that, Billy? Why wouldn't he keep her up at his ranch and feed her there?"

"'Cause he's a mean son of a bitch."

"I don't believe you. He wouldn't leave this calf out here. Not if he knew."

Billy feels sorry for me, I know, because he reaches his hand out and touches my shoulder. "She's tagged," he says.

Sure enough, the calf has a yellow tag hanging from her ear. X16. She turns her little white head as if to show it to me, as if to say, "See, I'm numbered, and who did this to me? Why do I hurt so much?"

I want to hold her. To tell her I don't understand, either. But if I move toward her, she'll have to take another painful, bloody step away. I'm the thing she's afraid of.

Billy's loading his .22. "Yep. If she lasted till weaning time, she'd bring a few hundred bucks. But now she's dying. Probably wandered too far from the windmill, trying to follow her mama. The cows went back to the water, and she couldn't keep up. Maybe her mama will come back, maybe not. I'm sure, though, I'm sure she's dying of thirst."

The calf bawls softly when he says that, like maybe she's agreeing. Then she folds her front legs and lays down on the ground and stretches out on her side. Her little belly heaves up into the sun and her tail twitches. Some flies rise up for a second, then settle on her again. Now I can see the pebbles and dirt matted to the bloody hair on the base of each stub.

She doesn't move when Billy slides a bullet into the chamber. She just lies there breathing, even when Billy raises the rifle and points it right behind her ear.

"You could get in a lot of trouble, Billy."

"Yeah," he says and unlocks the safety.

"Baxter knows she's out here."

He just shrugs his shoulders at that, and I don't want to be looking at him or his gun, so I look at her. The dirt in front of her pink nose springs into the air with each breath, her side heaves, an eyelid blinks slowly across a deep dark eye. She's a silky, soft form surrounded by all this yucca and cactus and dry grass. We all wait, Billy and I holding our breath and watching these puffs of dirt rise from the earth beneath her nose.

Billy lowers the gun. "I can't."

Before I know it, I'm hitting him, hard. "You do it, you son of a bitch," I hear myself yelling, and my fists are flying at him and Billy pushes me back and I fall into a yucca and scream as I scrape against needly barbs, and as I stand up the shot crashes out and the waves of sound splinter through me. Then everything's silent. Even that meadowlark's stopped singing.

I don't look at the calf's face. But I stare at the ground beneath her nose. There's blood streaming into it, dark and thick.

We're running toward our land, toward our trees. We fly alongside them and they scrape against our legs. Finally we stop and I'm trying to breathe, but I can't, really, because I'm crying and tired from running so far. Billy sets the rifle on the ground, and he's crying, too, but still he comes up and holds me. I press my forehead into his shirt and breathe in the warm air that smells like him. I want to stay like that for a long time, circled and protected by the arms of my brother, but all of a sudden, he jerks himself away. He raises his foot and stomps down on top of a tree, twists his foot and grinds the soft and brittle needles into dry ground. He reaches down and pulls at the tiny trunk. The tree stretches and then slowly gives way, followed by thin, curly roots pulling away from their home in the soil. Sandy grains of dirt sprinkle from their anchor and fall at our feet. The roots look like a bunch of tangled webs, and they're already wilting in the sun.

GRAYBLUE DAY

JACK'S NERVOUS. HE PUTS in a plug of chew, rests his elbows on his knees and his chin on his hands, and looks down at his cowboy boots. He wore his good gray ropers today, with his black Wranglers and silver belt buckle. That's how I can tell he's tense—I've never seen him dress up like this, not even for our first date.

This small park is surrounded by skyscrapers. In front of our bench is a water fountain, gurgling loud enough to compete with the traffic. The grass is cut low, the bushes are trimmed, and there are lines of marigolds shooting out in evenly spaced rows. I can appreciate this order; a grassy meadow with wildflowers and crooked paths would not do here. This city needs this park the way I need this city.

The only thing cluttering the park up is a swarm of pigeons. Their soft gray-blue is nice, but there are too many, flapping their wings, strutting, pecking at the sidewalk.

"We ain't got nothing for you," Jack says, looking at a few who have stepped close and cocked their heads. "Get gone."

This is what he says when he lets a cow out of the chute, or waves the horses into another pasture. "Get gone," he'll say, freeing a calf he's just roped, or to the horse he's just unsaddled. I imagine him leaning over me now and saying it to my stomach. "Get gone," he'd whisper, running his fingers below my belly button.

There's an hour until our appointment. I told Jack we'd get here too early, and then we'd just have to sit around and get nervous. But he had objections: he didn't know about parking, about rush hour, where the clinic was. The city, he said, was not his area of expertise.

We climbed into his truck while the sun was still rising. We wanted a full day in the city, is what I told my parents. A full day to shop, see the sights, go to the zoo, walk through a park eating a hotdog from one of those stands. In this imaginary day, the hours fly by. But this hour is holding on to each second before letting it go.

Jack spits. "Heard Marty Hibbs is selling out," he says. "Gonna get rid of his pigs. I might offer him eighty cents a pound for a few. Start a little business of my own."

"He's going to have an auction," I say, even though Jack already knows this. "Mom and I are going to look for antiques."

"Winnie, antique tractors is all he's likely to have."

"Maybe a dresser. Or a chest for my room."

Jack is not interested in dressers or chests, so he says, "Look at these folks." He nods at the fast-walking people on the sidewalk across the park. They're in business suits, mostly. No summer dresses, no jeans, no tanks and shorts here. I like watching the women's feet, their shoes. I like looking at their hair. Short cuts, or long but pulled up. Mine suddenly feels silly. But I consider: back home, just a few hours from here, it's not silly. Most every girl has long hair like mine, halfway down my back, pulled back with a silver barrette, and curled bangs. I realize I'm touching them now, and when I take my hand away my fingers feel sticky with hairspray.

"Different world," he says. He's being generous. In another mood, he would not be so kind. "Idiots," he'd say. "Don't know oatmeal comes from oats. Couldn't tell soybeans from alfalfa. Think hamburger just shows up in cellophane-wrapped chunks." That sort of thing. But not today. Today he looks at them with a kindness in his eye. Maybe because he's worn out from thinking about this thing. Or maybe because they're the ones with the clinic. We can grow good alfalfa, but we don't do certain medical procedures.

Jack runs his palms over his black Wranglers, and I look at my soft sweatpants and blue flannel shirt. I was going to dress up—it seemed somehow that I should.

But at the last minute my hand just reached out for these. They're comfortable and soft and familiar.

I pick a thread off the shirt and scratch my knees. Jack spits again and rubs his chin. We wait, staring out into this big city with light glinting off walls of glass and smooth granite stone, and then a small patch of red catches my eye. There, in the midst of all those pecking birds, is one that's got a piece of red string caught around its legs. Cinnamon-flavored dental floss, is what it looks like, tangled around both legs with just a small length in between. The bird can walk, but only in tiny, shuffling hop-steps. The pigeon looks like a shackled prisoner, walking all awkward like that.

I point and Jack grunts as he sees it, too. The pigeon is looking for bugs or crumbs right where the sidewalk meets grass. Each time it steps, it strains against the string, which is probably how the red tangle got so tightly wrapped in the first place. Occasionally it gets chased away by other birds and hobbles off, and sometimes pecks at its feet, flinging its head in the air. But I can see it's no use. That bird is never going to unwind all that string. We watch it hop and flutter and struggle for what seems like a very long time.

"Twenty minutes," I say finally. "Maybe we should start walking."

Jack nods, but he doesn't move. He spits his chew,

leans back, and tilts his face toward the sun. "It's noisy here."

There's a plane overhead and an ambulance siren, the bellow of traffic, this sputtering fountain. He can't think here, is what he means. There's no wind, no meadowlark, no tractor engine.

"Twenty minutes," I say. I feel sick all of a sudden. Too much noise, too much color.

Jack stands, so I stand, but he says, "Wait a minute," and pushes me gently back down onto the bench.

We can't wait, I'm about to tell him. I'm getting too far along. It's time to get gone. I think he's about to face me, and we'll have this conversation all over again, weighing our choices, trying to be certain, talking and hoping all our talk will reveal an answer that isn't there. But instead Jack turns away from me and walks, real slow, up to that bird.

The other pigeons shuffle or flutter away, making room for him in a lazy kind of way. The shackled bird hops out of the way along with the others. But Jack's hand darts out at the last minute and catches it, right above the wings. I've seen him catch a chicken that way: slow, slow, and then one fast dart.

He brings the bird back and holds it against his thigh with one hand while he leans to the side and reaches into his pocket for his knife with his other. He unfolds the small blade with his thumb, turns the bird on its back, and cuts the string between the bird's legs. He unravels each side till he's got two red tangles on his lap. The pigeon lies still under Jack's hand, still except for its chest moving up and down and fast blinks of its deep dark eye.

Jack tosses the bird into the air. The pigeon flutters down a few feet ahead of us and stands for a moment. It takes a few small steps, tilts to the side as if it might stumble, and then starts walking around, calm as can be.

"Get gone," I say. But I say it more to what's just flooded into my mind: I wouldn't have thought of saving that bird. Maybe I couldn't have caught it, but I didn't even try. Didn't even think of trying. Blank, I am. Blank and cold and nothing, and that's something to fear. My mind doesn't have such things occur to it, much less see the options.

Jack did, though. Jack saw and considered. So I grab on to his hand, the one that was just holding the bird, and I squeeze. If only I can hear from him one more time that this is right.

"Look at that bird," he says. "It's walking around like normal, as if it's already forgotten that trouble."

It's true. The bird shows no sign that it's stretching its legs for the first time in a long time. Already, it has returned to pecking for crumbs.

"That was a nice thing you did, Jack," I say. "Now nothing is holding it back."

To prove this to us, maybe, the pigeon lifts and flies away. We watch as it darts up and around the corner of a building made of glinting glass.

"You ready?" There's a tightness in Jack's voice, one that tells me he's not. He'd be content to go back home, to face it all.

I'm still holding on to his hand, and I think of how fast that hand moved, charging out and covering that bird. I realize there wasn't much consideration or deliberation after all. Just a quick act. Slow, slow, one fast dart—it's the only way some things get done.

RATTLESNAKE FIRE

THE WILDFIRE TURNED UNEXPECTEDLY and in the opposite direction predicted. This left the ranchers up high with barely enough time to spraypaint their phone numbers on their horses. They cut fences, opened gates, and whooped the cattle and horses out, trying to direct them into the roads and creek beds that would guide them down the mountain. Stock trailers were loaded with the best belongings, and as men and women and children abandoned their ranches and drove away, they sent sparks of wishes into the air: that unbranded calves would stay with their mamas, that instinct would lead the animals down to safety, that nature would show some pity and preserve all that they had worked for.

Those downslope, the ones who had more time, put out a call for help. This call was repeated on the radio and was what Ben heard instead of the usual morning farm report. He sat at his kitchen table waiting for his sister, Anita, to come out of the guest bedroom, which she might not do for a couple of hours, and listened to the plea for anyone with a stock trailer to meet at the school parking lot to help evacuate animals. As he stared into his coffee, he decided that he would not go.

"What I'd like to see is a stream of stock trailers, one right after the other, climbing up that mountain pass," the radio announcer said. "Every time I hear the national anthem, my heart jumps up and salutes. That's how I'd feel to see such a sight. You know that feeling, I'm sure you do, so get out there and lend a helping hand. There's an estimated one thousand head up there, so it's gonna take nearly a hundred trips to get those animals out."

Ben sipped his coffee. He figured Eddie was on his way up there already. They'd spoken of the fire this morning over at the donut shop, shrugging off the most recent tally of how many structures were lost and wincing at the report that a cluster of cattle had been engulfed in flames.

"I know whatcha mean," the waitress had said to their response. "A cow worth a couple a hundred bucks is harder to take than all them million-dollar houses being burnt up, isn't it?"

You bet it is, they agreed. The livestock and wild game—well, that was a shame. So was the plight of the ranchers, with all that fence to rebuild, outbuildings and ranch homes and corrals—Jesus, all that work—as if ranching wasn't hard enough. Also, they felt sorry for the hippies, the ones that lived up the canyon in small A-frames they built themselves to escape the rest of humankind, which was something Ben and Eddie could surely sympathize with. What they didn't find hard to take was the loss of the glass-and-wood cabins cluttering up the mountainside for the rich folks' weekends away from Denver. Ben wasn't sorry to see those houses burnt to a crisp. Serves 'em right, he said, to which Eddie agreed, adding that those folks probably needed some trauma and heartbreak in what he imagined were their otherwise soft-hand lives. That's what Eddie called folk like that, Soft-Hands.

They weren't naive enough to discount the fact that they felt sorrier for the people most like themselves—humans are apt to do that, is what Ben said to Eddie, who nodded and said, "Ain't that the truth." But no matter what they thought, he added, nature had more rights than people and their too-fancy homes—more rights than anybody, in fact—and it was good of her to give a reminder once in a while, to put humans in their place.

Well, he wouldn't go. Heck with it all, he thought, which was the same thing he'd been thinking a lot recently. He didn't feel good, for one thing, and only in the last few months had it become clear that it's nearly impossible to care about anything when the body aches. He knows that his aches are minor on the scale of human suffering, and yet they're enough to make him feel drained. His stomach's been bothering him, and not the little sort of tummyache the idiot doctor thinks he's talking about, but the serious unbearable pain of a heavy weight lodged beneath his ribs.

Anita thinks it's cancer, and he's relieved that his sister, at least, takes his complaints seriously—Renny and everyone else advise Tums, which makes him want to shake them by the neck. But it's not cancer; he's been checked for that. Just a failing of the stomach, a weakening of the muscle. He's supposed to eat bland foods and sip at tea and forgo the alcohol. These are not changes he's prepared to make, but he soon will in order to get some relief. He needs to remove the physical pain crushing him and claw himself out of this stupor.

Ben pulled the morning paper and a pen toward him. In the margin he meant to make a list of the things he should do. Instead he stared at the fringe of the thin paper until he heard Anita, who was stirring in the extra bedroom. She shuffled into the kitchen in her white robe and slumped into a chair beside him.

The fact that she got up so late every morning was the cause of a sheepishness she projected until he said what she wanted him to, which was, "What the hell, it's your vacation." So he said it, and she perked up, her head lifted with the poise and aloofness he was used to.

She'd told him she'd flown out to Colorado to see her big brother, but it was clear the visit had more to do with escaping something in Boston. A tiny part of him hoped that was the case; he admitted he was glad to see her suffer a bit. But no, maybe such a wish was just the result of his hurt feelings. She'd never had much interest in the brother who stayed home and ranched instead of going to an east-coast college, who hadn't married rich (Anita's husband was the king of the Soft-Hands, Ben told Eddie), the misfit brother who didn't care much about fashion or the conveniences of life.

She'd only written a handful of times in all the years she'd been gone, never acknowledged the birthday cards he sent her, and only made a brief and quiet appearance at his daughter's funeral. Only once, soon after she'd moved back east, had she called and invited him to come visit. He'd gone, even though he knew what she wanted, which was the chance to show off her beautiful, clean, fancy home. To show him she'd come quite a way, with which he could only agree. She wanted something more from him, then, some recognition that she was the better person for the life she had made. This he refused to give. In his comments and compliments, he refused to say that she and her life were superior to his, that days spent in an office were better than those on a tractor, that a new leather couch was better than a dog-hair-covered old one. He refused to say this because although she hoped it to be true, he knew it was not.

She was here because she wanted something again, though he wasn't sure what. He suspected something had worn thin in her life, that the heat that prodded her on was dissipating. And he couldn't help suspecting that she'd come to comfort herself with his discomfort, to measure the distance between them again.

He wasn't all that interested in obliging her this time either. But he slid a coffee cup over to her and filled it. She mumbled a thank-you, and they sat quiet for a while, until Anita said, "Oh," and tilted her head toward the radio. He hadn't been listening any longer, but he realized she had been, and her face had taken on a look of concern. He scowled and looked away. He was disgusted with her, with the radio announcer, with the whole human race for this fake concern. She felt nothing for these ranchers and animals, and why should she? It was a rare case when people cared about things they were unconnected to.

He saw that he was right. He watched her face flit between concern and interest and then back to self-centered sleepiness, and she never once lifted her eyes to him with an inquiring look, wondering if they should answer the call for help. What she finally said was, "Will the fire get here?"

"No."

"Are you sure?"

"Yes. I guess I should go up there, but I'm not feeling so good today."

"Did you take your medicine?"

"No."

"Why not?"

"It doesn't work."

"It *should* work. That's what it's for. I think you should see another doctor. That's what I'll do today. I'll make you another appointment. Is that all right with you?"

He didn't say anything, but he felt himself rock a bit with assent, and then felt her surprise.

"Okay, then." She shuffled off in her slippers to his desk in the living room, and he was left to listen to the reports of the fire, of wind shifts, of the crew's weariness. Goddamn, he should go up and help, he knew it. Well, if he could muster the energy to go, he'd tell whoever was in charge that he was willing to haul cattle and work-horses, but not any expensive Arabians or city kids' ponies. And if given grief about it, he'd tell them to hell with it. He'd say he ought to be raking his hay to get it baled before the rain came, the rain so desperately needed and that everyone wanted except for the few like him who had their grass cut and needed dry weather till it was baled. Cattle or workhorses, he'd say again, that's all I'll do. Otherwise I'm going to go sit on my tractor and rake hay and hope for dry weather, because the heck with all of you.

It was because of Anita, he knew, that he hated the rich out of proportion to what made sense, perhaps because he equated her wealth with her neglect. What he wanted, of course, was some acknowledgment of *his* life. Something about how gorgeous the landscape was, how hard he worked, how relaxed and easy he was on a horse. How *he,* at least in some respects, was the one with the life worth coveting.

If she did say such a thing, he'd go ahead and admit that she'd been brave to leave the ranch, to learn about and build a new life. But they were too different now to try to appreciate and understand the other in the sort of way that takes effort and time—no, he doubted if either of them had enough strength and energy for that now.

When the call came, he wasn't surprised much. As he listened to Eddie yelling over the buzz of his cell phone and the bawling of cattle, Ben looked at his sister, sitting on the couch hunched over the yellow pages opened to "Physicians." He glanced toward the kitchen window that faced the mountains, which was the direction

Eddie was calling from. A billowing cloud of dark smoke rose like a mushroom cloud above a far slope of pine trees and spread like a fan in the air.

"I'm at the After-Math Ranch," Eddie was saying. "Ted Austen's place. You know where it is?"

"I was on my way up anyway. Just now. I'll drive straight up." That's what he said, but he wanted to say that he'd just had it with this world, and didn't anyone else get like that, just fed up and tired? Didn't they ever get to a point where they couldn't even get shamed into caring, because there was just nothing nothing nothing inside?

He left Anita curled up and hugging herself, and went outside and backed his pickup up to the red stock trailer. He rubbed his stomach and ate a handful of Tums, a bottle of which rattled around with all the other junk on the seat. Just as he was pulling away, Anita came running out, waving for him to stop. She was dressed, now, wearing jeans and a white T-shirt and ball cap.

"I want to come," she said. "If I'd known you were going, I would have asked to come along."

He regarded her for a minute. "Why?"

"Oh, Ben, who knows." She walked to the passenger side and opened the door. "Can I come or what?"

He reached out his hand to help pull her into the truck, and then, so that his frustration might dissipate, he began to talk. "We're going to the After-Math Ranch. A retired math professor owns it. Get it? But it has another meaning, too, because 'after-math' is the stubble after a crop's been cut."

"Clever. It might have a third meaning after this fire." She laughed and, perhaps because she feared her comment was not appropriate, she grew solemn. "I hope not, though."

"Oh hell." He was surprised by the edge in his voice, and was relieved when Anita laughed again.

"I should care, shouldn't I?" She rubbed her temples and closed her eyes. "I'm having a hard time caring about anything these days."

Here's where they were still a bit alike, that's what he wanted to say then, but before he could form the words, she was talking again. "Every once in a while people surprise me," she said. "Look at this."

Ahead of them was a line of trailers that wound up the canyon as far as they could see, a couple miles at least, he figured, of pickups and trailers back-to-back. The sight *did* make his throat feel tight with pride, mostly because he could show off this bit of generosity to his sister. "We got horse people," he said, lifting his finger off the steering wheel and pointing to a fancy new trailer in front of them, which was being pulled by a matching truck, both painted with swirls of turquoise. "And we got cattle people." Now he pointed at the trailer in front of it, a beat-up brown thing that looked much like his own.

"Money," she said.

"Yep," he said, and then, "I don't believe a rich and poor person can be true friends."

"And if someone thinks they can, I bet you it's the richer person who thinks so." She laughed. "Oh, Ben, I can see that, even from where I'm at."

He felt a sudden surge of gratitude. Her words weren't much, really, but after all these years of almost nothing, they seemed like enough.

They didn't speak much the rest of the drive, and it was the radio announcer who kept the silence from being difficult. The information his animated voice conveyed was interesting to them both, simply because it was new, and perhaps because it involved pain for someone else. Before evacuating houses, the announcer said, homeowners should put a sprinkler on the roof, cut away trees and brush, dig a ditch, pull up all the plants. "It's called a defensible space, folks," said the announcer. "Create this space if you have the time."

"Defensible space," Anita said. "That's a fine idea." Then, "That's something I should tell Richard about."

He could have told her that he understood—he'd just been thinking about Renny, how they'd moved apart for that reason, for just a bit more space. Instead he looked out the window at the river curling alongside the road. Usually there were rafters and kayakers, folks fly-fishing and families having picnics, but now the river was deserted and there was only the water, tumbling down rocks and pooling near the banks. But it was the sky that caught his attention when they rounded a corner. Ahead was the billowing cloud of gray smoke, a dark smudge against the backdrop of a bright blue sky.

"There's our Rattlesnake Fire," she said. The news station had dubbed it that, since so many firefighters had experienced run-ins with snakes. And also, at the beginning, the fire had spread out in a zigzag, like a snake lying in the sun.

"You ever been bit by a snake, Anita?"

"No. One of those life experiences I'll never have."

"I got bit a couple of years back. Surprised a rattlesnake, and he just zapped up and got me quicker than lightning." This is one of the many stories he would have liked to have told her soon after it happened. He had practiced telling her the story in his mind, and when he told Eddie and Renny and Carolyn about it, he imagined he was telling Anita instead. It was silly of him to want to impress her with stories and know-how, like he had way back when he'd put the worm on her hook or had her big-eyed at the story of a mountain lion he'd seen—those times when they'd clung together because they were two lonely ranch kids with a lot of work to do and not much to make them feel special. Crazy, a grown man still wanting acknowledgment, interest, love from his sister. But Anita was looking out the window and didn't seem all that interested in his story, so he concentrated on the road ahead and let the silence seep between them.

The radio announcer was describing the county fairgrounds, filled with rescued livestock. Ranchers from all over the state were offering free pasture for animals, free hay, opening their homes to displaced folks. "It's not Rattlesnake Fire that's such a sight to see," the announcer said. "It's the people swarming to help, that's the thing worth noticing here."

When Ben pulled into the After-Math Ranch, an old trailer was already backed up to the corral, and Eddie and another man were pushing the back door closed on a load of cattle. Ben let his truck idle until the other driver, whom he didn't recognize, drove away. Each man lifted his fingers off the steering wheel in a muted wave as they passed one another. Then Ben backed up his own trailer, following Eddie's gestures.

When Ben climbed out of the truck, he was surprised by the strength of the smell. The air didn't look particularly smoky, although bits of ash floated past his eyes, but the smell of scorched earth was strong. The cows in the corral were bawling, and there was a distant buzz of airplanes and whine of helicopters. The hot sunlight and the noise made him feel dizzy. He leaned against the pickup for a moment, bowing his head to regain his balance.

"Glad you came."

"I was on my way."

"Ted took my truck down awhile ago. I told him I'd stay and load the rest of the cows for as long as I could. You should have seen him, Ben."

Eddie's face was full of sweat—there were so many little rivulets of moisture that Ben was struck with a sudden worry for him. He reached into his truck for a jug of water and handed it to Eddie, who tilted it up above him, letting the water flow first into his mouth and then across his face. "You don't look so good yourself," Ben said.

"Ted looked like he was about to keel over. He's been working round the clock."

"Hard for him to leave, I reckon."

"He wanted to stay, but the last thing someone needs to see is his life burned up. I made the whole family go, take my truck down. Do you think I did right?"

"Sure," Ben said, but only because he had no other words to offer, and because he wasn't sure whether it was better to stand strong and fight a futile battle or get the hell out. If he knew that, he'd know what to do with Renny, with Anita, with his life.

"Guess we better get a move on," Eddie said. "This'll be the last load. They told us to get out twenty minutes ago. Fire's close for sure, but I don't think we're in any real danger."

"Naw." Ben turned to follow Eddie toward the pens, but then stopped and turned toward Anita, to see, perhaps, if he had her consent to stay, or if she was frightened, or to see if she had been listening at all.

She was still sitting in the truck, looking toward the house and the barn behind it. She turned, then, perhaps knowing he was looking for an answer. "Don't worry," she said and shrugged, "I don't have the energy to be worried."

As Ben and Eddie rounded up the cattle, Ben heard the slam of the truck's door. Anita was walking toward the house, cocking her head and looking uncertain. She emerged a moment later carrying a small coffee table, then later with a painting and a quilt, all of which she loaded into the bed of the truck. Soon she was walking quickly between house and truck, running almost, and for a moment she did not look like a well-cared-for woman, someone who lived in a house that cost as much as his entire ranch, but someone who was afraid, who was working hard out of necessity and fear, laboring for survival. As he *he-yaawd* at the cattle and flapped his arms at the cows who tried to back out of the trailer, he watched her jog, faster and faster, from house to truck. On one trip, she emerged from the house with something that looked like an old sewing machine table, which looked similar to one their mother had owned. Anita was bowed backwards with the weight of it but still walked as fast as she could, jerking and stumbling, and he wanted to rush and help her. He couldn't, though; he was leaning against a cow's rear to encourage her to step up into the trailer, and if he let up on the pressure, the cattle would turn and bolt. He could only watch and wince as Anita strained under the weight, frightened by the way she lurched toward the truck.

Just as Ben was pushing the trailer door shut, a calf darted, slipping away between two fence poles. As he and Eddie dodged around the corral trying to get her in, Ben remembered his grandfather telling him about the war, how the worst part was the screaming of a colt that had its back legs blown off. They had agreed that humans could inflict whatever evils they desired on each other, but that animals ought to be left out of it. Some animals screamed, and some suffered silently and dumbly, which was how he imagined the death of two cows who'd gotten stuck in a ditch and frozen last winter. Humans did that, screamed or suffered silently, maybe depending on the situation or the individual soul. Oh Jesus, how he'd like to tell Anita that he was sorry she had pain going on inside her. He'd say, I got some of my own troubles too.

We seem to be the quiet sort, or quiet is what our particular distress calls for, who knows, but we're hurting anyhow, aren't we?

He felt sick, still. The smell of diesel from his truck mixed with the smoke, and his stomach felt empty and he wished he had taken in a bit less coffee this morning. He should have slept in a little later, like his sister, instead of rising with the sun. Most of all, he wished he could sit down, just for a minute, in some cool, quiet place.

Ben forced the last calf in, pressing her against the others already in the trailer. The cows bawled and kicked, and the ones on the edges put their noses out of the slats and snorted as the men pushed the back door closed behind them.

"It's for your own damn good," Eddie grunted as he locked the back of the trailer. "We're trying to save your ugly asses."

Ben chuckled. "You gonna ride back with us, or face the fire and the snakes?"

"I'll take a ride with you, if you'll have me," Eddie said. "I already opened the gates for whatever cows are left. Let's get the hell out of here."

They both stood for a moment, catching their wind and wiping sweat from their faces. Ben was hot clear through, and he couldn't tell if the heat came from him or if the fire was getting closer, but in any case, he wanted to get away, get down to his ranch and sit by the coolness of the river. As he walked to the front of the truck, he could see that Anita had loaded up quite a bit. Plants and rugs and boxes full of knickknacks were coated in a thin layer of ash, which, when he looked up, he could see falling like snowflakes from the sky. As he climbed in the truck beside her, he saw that the hair on her brow was wet, and she too was sucking in air in an effort to catch her breath. She was staring at a lamp in her lap, one that looked like it was made of stained glass.

"Nice of you," he said, nodding at the lamp.

She nodded but didn't speak. He thought she looked on the verge of tears, and so he busied himself with starting the truck. She had to move closer to him to make room for Eddie, who squeezed in on the other side. "Watch out for these," she said as she moved closer. She nodded at a jumble of animal figurines dressed up in fancy clothes. They were crammed into the seat between them, and Ben considered, for a brief instant, what sort of strange world produced porcelain rabbits in hoop skirts and how they came to be staring up at him from a seat littered with bits of hay and pieces of cows' ear tags and baling twine.

As he drove away from the After-Math Ranch and turned onto the main road, he saw the billowing smoke of Rattlesnake Fire in his rearview mirror. Where smoke met land, an orange glow bloomed into the air. The truck was heavy with cattle, and he had to shift to a lower gear and concentrate on the curves. They passed a police car heading up the canyon with its sirens going, then caught up with the line of trailers snaking down the mountain with horses' tails or cows' sides showing through the back doors and side windows.

Anita held the lamp with one hand and rubbed at her eyes with the other, and Eddie kept wiping the moisture from his forehead. After a while, though, Ben felt their breath even and their bodies cool, and now they were listening not to their pounding hearts, but to the sound of porcelain animals clinking against one another and the cattle bawling from the trailer.

"Tonight there'll be quite a sunset," Ben said. "Sad to think of it that way, isn't it? But that smoke will make the sunset so red, all that red above those blue mountains."

"I didn't think of that," Anita said.

"That's what this fire's taught me," he said. "That devastation looks pretty damn good from afar."

She laughed, then, and with her laughter there seemed to be some sort of surrender, some release of a tightness within her. She said, "You got that right. So the least we can do is pull up lawn chairs and watch it."

"All right," he agreed. "That's a fine idea." He gave

one last look in his rearview mirror, at the fire that was chasing livestock and wild game and humans down the canyon. Things that should never come close were being funneled together, and he wondered whether such a moment could save them as they fled down the mountain.

A NEW NAME EACH DAY

I WISH MOM WOULD say something, but instead she just stands, hands on hips, and looks in the opposite direction from Billy and Ray, who are drinking water from an old milk jug. That's something I discovered about her once. How she gets back at you by pretending you aren't worth noticing.

"Rachel's driving this time," Ray says, taking Mom's hand and leading her to the pickup. He's making her drive because I let the truck lurch around too much. He's been yelling at me about it all day, about letting the clutch out smoother, because he says it's like riding a bucking bronc up there. He's been standing in the bed of the truck, stacking the hay bales that Billy throws up, grunting and yelling as I pitch us down this endless field between rows of hay.

Mom climbs in the driver's side and I sit in the passenger seat, but still she doesn't look my way. She hasn't looked at me since yesterday, which was my thirteenth birthday, which was when Ray told her to get out of her Damn Slump and do something for me. I told her I wanted a picnic. Instead we had what she called Special Wild Meal, which was everything Ray and Billy had shot and stuck in the freezer: a duck, a pheasant, an ugly fish Billy caught up at the dam. There wasn't even a cake, and the birds had bits of shot and feathers still in them. We ate on the couches, instead of on a blanket spread in a field, and our couches aren't even really couches; they're more like huge pillows resting on frames. We got them free because they were sitting by the side of the road, and they smell like cat pee.

When Billy asked if he could be excused and go outside, I asked too. Mom rolled her eyes at me because I didn't eat much, but she shrugged and said I could do what I wanted on my birthday as long as I brought her a beer, which I did Without An Argument. On my way back from the kitchen, I heard Ray say something about getting a bit of quiet time, and he was sliding his hand up her leg, and she was smiling, so I knew we'd be outside for a while. But before I went, I said, "Thanks for nothing." I didn't bother to wait around to see what look she shot back at me, which I guess is why she won't look at me now.

Before Billy climbs in the bed of the truck, he leans in and bonks me on the head. "Hey Cuckaburra," he says to me. "Happy day after birthday." Cuckaburra is his name for me today. Yesterday it was Ornery Toad. Each day he gives me another name, the first word that pops into his head when he sees me. Tomorrow it might be Iguana or it might be Wily Monster, who knows, but it will make me smile.

Mom's smiling a bit now too, and she's a better driver than I am, that's for sure. She lets out the clutch and guides the pickup forward between the rows of hay, smooth as can be. She's cheered up some, and now she's singing along with the radio, some country song. Even driving and singing, and she's still able to watch Ray, who is now throwing the bales up to Billy. In the rearview mirror, she watches him walk toward each bale, watches his old gloves grasp orange baling twine, watches his back arch as he sends the bale spiraling into the air and into the bed of the truck. She sees dust and hay fall back onto his red face as he throws the bale up, sees him move on to the next one, and she lets the truck go just enough to keep up with him.

"Why he works so hard," Mom says, keeping an eye on him but leaning over to whisper to me, "is because he wants things so bad. There is no half-wanting about him."

There's nothing to say to that. I watch her hands on the steering wheel. She's painted her fingernails a burnt orange with white drops of polish on top to make flowers. She's always trying stuff like that, making herself pretty in ways that make no sense. Already the polish is chipped and the flowers look ugly, like they're sad to be on fingernails instead of in a field rising up to the sun.

"I, on the other hand, am a half-wanter," she says. "Sometimes being that way makes things easier but sometimes harder because you're pretty much satisfied with anything and sometimes that can lead to trouble. But this wanting part of Ray, I understand. You've got it too, Jess. You both want that land so bad it's choking you up."

She's talking about yesterday, when Ray promised to give me what I want most. Next birthday, he said, we'll all be living on our own section away from this rented house with its piles of junk, away from where we are, which he says, and I agree, is a white-trash house on somebody else's land. We're going to build a house together and settle down and be a family and watch sunsets on the porch. He winked at me and presented me with a certificate for my very own acre, to do with what I want, and he said to start dreaming about the possibilities right away.

Then he leaned over and kissed my mom and said, "Isn't that right, Rachel? Do you dream of sunsets too?"

When he says her name I think of how she told me once, long ago when she was drunk, that she wasn't quite satisfied with the name Rachel and she wasn't quite satisfied with the name Mom. She wanted, she said, to be a little bit more than either of them. She said that's the reason for so many boyfriends. Some of them called her Rachel, and some called her Little Bird or Honey or Sweet Gal. I learned what they called her, and I learned their names too. I learned about different-colored toothbrushes and different preferences for brands of beer. And then I learned about Ray, whom I thought was different because him she actually married. She must have loved him enough to move to this place in the middle of nowhere Colorado, away from the mountains and away from our grandparents. But it is not enough, I see that now. Because yesterday when Ray asked her about sunsets and our some-day house, she said, "Yes, yes, it's enough to make up a dream," but the way she said it made us all grow quiet.

So maybe there will be no house. My mom has a greasy old magnet pinned to the refrigerator that reads, "Mom Is Another Name For Love." I'm just starting to realize that maybe that's not always true.

Yesterday, after Billy and I were excused from the Special Wild Meal, he invited me into his Hideout. That's Billy for you, I was thinking, giving better names to things than they deserve. His hideout is just a place in last year's haystack where two bales fell out near the bottom but the rest of the stack stayed up, so there's a little place to crawl into. The only neat thing about his hideout, I told him, is something he doesn't even know about. As we climb in, I tell him the story. How last summer I was climbing around and found where the chicken made a nest and laid her eggs, in the same place we were sitting. Remember, I said, how Mom was all mad because she thought the chicken wasn't laying eggs at all, which is what she'd bought her for? But I learned that chicken was just smart. Instead of getting her egg taken away each morning, she just took off and found someplace new. I told that chicken I was going to follow her example someday, but in the meantime I'd keep her nest a secret. I was hoping there'd be some chicks following her around one day, which would surprise everyone but me, but that's not what happened. One morning there was just a bunch of feathers near the haystack and the chicken and eggs were gone.

"So that," I said to Billy, "is what you get for trying to get away."

But Billy was not interested in my story. What he was interested in, he said, was getting a rabbit. I just rolled my eyes at that. Partly because he'd never get one, and partly because Billy doesn't understand that most people don't want to eat rabbits, especially ones they shoot, and

that I don't want to, either. He doesn't seem to understand that we're poor.

I was thinking about everyone else at their birthday
parties with decorated tables and food without bits of
shot, and I was just about to fall asleep when I felt Billy
tense up and raise his gun. He was pointing it at a little
gray dove. The dirt was ground into a fine dust next to
the haystack, and wherever the bird hopped it left perfect prints, each one shaped like three little prongs. It
was pecking at the hay scattered on the ground and then
hopping and pecking some more.

"Billy, don't," I whispered, and at the same time, the
dove looked up, maybe hearing the danger that was
coming its way. The crack of the gun went off at the
same time the bird lifted its wings to fly. It climbed a
little into the air, mostly sideways, and then fell, flutter-
ing, to the ground.

"Got it!" Billy slipped out of the hideout and grabbed
the dove. He turned around to face me and at first he
was smiling, but then a sick look came across his face.
The dove in his hand was blinking its eye, and one wing
stretched out, trying to make flight.

"Kill it, Billy!" I kept saying it over and over, but he
just stood there, looking at the bird twisting in his palm.
I ran up to him and grabbed the bird from his hands.
I was surprised by how light it was and how warm and

soft those feathers were. They were like touching silky dust on a smooth board, and I wish that's what I could have known about that bird, but what I knew was that I had to kill it, so I twisted the bird's head until I heard a snap.

I would like to tell Mom about it now, how I punched Billy until he cried, how I told him that he was no damn hunter if he couldn't even kill the bird he'd hurt. But also that I didn't mean it like Ray does. I meant that Billy is Billy and Billy was never meant to be a hunter. How I keep trying to show him that, which is why, as I suddenly realized it myself, I told him that we don't have to love Ray, and we don't even have to love Mom.

What is the name for it, he'd said after punching me back, when it's not love and not hate? And what about them loving us?

I said I didn't know, but that we should go bury that bird. He was cradling the soft gray dove in his open palms, like he was offering it up to someone. I took the bird in one hand and took his hand with my other and led him to the barn. I got the shovel and walked back outside and started to dig, and I said, Let's bury this bird before we forget who we are.

I'm trying to figure out how to tell Mom this, to give her a warning that it's about to go one way or the other. Billy and I are either going to move toward her or away from her, and she better do something soon if she wants us together.

What I guess is that Ray's been basically asking her the same thing, because I can see he wants her, too. We all want her in a whole-wanting way, and if we don't get it, I think we're all bound to turn away.

I'm trying to figure out the words to tell her this when I hear a half-scream, half-yelp coming from Ray. I turn my head to see out the window. He's standing back from a bale, looking at a small snake that has been smashed in with the grass.

Billy's laughing from where he's standing in the bed of the truck, saying check out this damned old snake. Mom and I step out of the truck to get a better view.

"It's not a rattler," Mom says. "Just a cute garter. Surprised you, didn't it?"

But Ray's not listening. He's still looking at the snake. Half of the snake sticks out, twisting in the air. The other half is caught under baling twine and compacted hay.

"Cut the twine," Mom says, throwing Ray the pocketknife that had been resting on the seat between us.

I'm looking at that crazy snake, wondering how it got caught in the bale like that, so I don't see Ray until he's walking in front of the truck toward Mom. What I see is a pace that's too fast, a face that's too red. What I hear is something about wasting a bale for a goddamn snake, about her being so smart that she can get it out herself.

Mom laughs. I hear the surprised snort escape her throat a second before I hear the slap that cracks against her face. Ray's pulling her away from the truck, pushing her down in the grass. His boot lands on the back of her thigh, and she flies forward from its force, and I hear myself saying "Hey!" in surprise. I'm looking for Billy, but out of the corner of my eye I see Mom's neck snap when Ray's palm cracks into her head. I don't know whether to run to Mom or away from her, so I cover my ears and sink down into the field and curl my back so that my head is touching clumped bundles of grass. A motionless bug is poised in the place where blade turns to root. I keep my eyes on it while I hear Mom screaming "You bastard!" over and over. Then she's not screaming anymore, and I'm just hearing the noise of his fist hitting her. I cover my face after that, hold my chin against my chest and breathe in the smell of my sweat and bits of hay, and I stay there, stay with that smell, until I hear it get quiet.

I look up to see Ray dragging Mom toward the snake. She jerks out of his grip as they near, and without even hesitating she reaches out and grabs the snake right below its head with her thumb and forefinger. With her other hand, she pulls on the tight baling twine. It looks like that snake's going to tear in half as it stretches with her pull. Seems like forever, this snake stretching between the bale and my mother, between green grass and blue sky.

The snake slides out and hangs from her hand, coiling in the air. Mom walks away from us, holding it away from her. She means to put that snake in the grass and let it go. But before she sets it down, she turns to Ray. "You asshole," she says. "All fucked up over a goddamn garter snake."

It's then that I notice the blood running down her face, and it's then that I notice Ray moving toward her again in a way that makes me close my eyes. But right then I hear the sound of Billy's feet running, and all of us turn to look at him.

He's got the rifle from the house and is pointing it at Ray. He slows as he reaches us and keeps his eyes on Ray as he walks toward Mom. She drops the snake, and the blades of grass move as it disappears. Then Mom takes the rifle with the same hand. She puts the butt of it against her shoulder.

Blood is really streaming now, from her nose to chin, and from her ear to her neck. She's shaking so bad it looks like she's about to crack apart.

"Billy and Jess, get in the truck," she says.

Then Ray starts talking. "Fucking bitch," is what he says first. But then he throws down the pocketknife, which I guess was in his hand all this time, and he starts talking slower. "Rachel, Rachel. I'm sorry." He says her name over again, soft and quiet, then something about how goddamn hot it is today, words about the heat and the snake.

Billy is pushing me toward the truck and we climb in and watch Mom walk around Ray, toward the driver's side. She slides the gun in first, across our legs, then pulls herself in. Her leg touches mine and I want to crawl into that touch, curl myself up, and press against her.

Only when we're on the county road does she make a sound. It's a gasp and then a choking kind of cry, and then Billy and I are crying too. She says our names over and over, says it's going to be all right. Finally she pulls over on the side of a wheat field and turns off the ignition. I want her to tell me again that it's okay, to tell me that we're safe. Instead, she takes the gun from our laps. She steps from the truck and walks a few paces away and then turns around.

"You going to help me unload this?" She's asking Billy, who doesn't answer. He's looking straight ahead out the windshield. It's just like something she might do, refusing to take notice at all.

"I don't know how to unload it," she says.

Still he doesn't say anything, so she looks away from him, toward the wheat. "I'll shoot the damn bullets out, then," she says. She puts the stock against her shoulder, aims to where golden wheat meets blue sky, and turns off the safety. There is a moment of stillness, and then the shots ring out past all of us, echoing into all that nothing.

We are the children my mom did not want, from a man she did not want to marry. She kept us but left him. Then she got a boyfriend, boyfriend, boyfriend, boyfriend, and then Ray. I'm looking in the direction that the bullets just flew and thinking that there must be names for different kinds of love but that true love must be the whole-wanting sort, and I'm guessing I do love her after all.

Mom climbs back into the truck and we sit, silent, staring out at the sky until it darkens into a smooth steel blue. When she starts the truck up, I feel sick. I don't feel like talking but I have to know, so I whisper, "Can you tell me where we're going?"

She lets out the clutch and guides the pickup onto the road. "Home," she says. At first I think she means to Ray. But instead of driving away from the mountains, she's driving toward them. Then I realize she means her home, the ranch where she grew up. Maybe she believes, like I do, that there's only a small amount of time when we can start again each day, new, and that such a thing is still possible if we hurry and move on together underneath this dimming sky.

THE RECORD KEEPER

MY MOTHER LEANS AGAINST the corral fence, explaining to my cousin Jess about prolapses and how the best thing to do is to shove the uterus back in and sew the cow up with thick string and give her a shot of penicillin. "Once the birth canal is back inside the cow," she says, "you use a big hook needle and make purse-string stitches. So, do you want me to teach you to sew?"

"I don't think so," Jess says.

My brother, Jack, tries to make Jess cringe by offering details. "The uterus is heavy and slick and it takes two people, one to hold it up, and the other to punch it back inside," he says. "It slimes you all over."

But Jess doesn't scrunch her face, as I did when I was her age. Instead, she nods in delight, and says that although she would never wish that on any mama cow, if it's going to happen anyway, she'd like to be there to see it.

Dad and Jack climb over the fence into the pen

crowded with cattle and start arguing about which bull's semen to use next year. Jack scratches a yearling heifer on the hump between her ears, and when the animal raises her head to sniff his shirt, she leaves a smudge of mucus on his sleeve. Jack eyes the snot in an offhand way and then an ornery look floods his face. He leans over during the height of the argument and wipes the slime on Dad's cheek. Dad scowls and rubs it back onto Jack. He slugs Jack softly in the belly, and then Jack punches Dad, and then they box each other, shuffling around in the manure like they're in a ring, quick jabs and ducks to the side. The cows press against the railing, watching the circling boxers with sleepy interest, flicking their tails against the flies.

"I've about had it with you hooligans," Jess sings out, mimicking my father. "I'm growing impatient with your childishness." Strands of blond hair lit by the sun shoot up from yesterday's braids. She's wearing blue shorts and red cowboy boots and there's two slices of leg in between.

I wonder if anyone realizes how much I see. If anyone notices how I watch Dad and Jack laugh as they give up boxing and wave and whoop at the cows, how my mother stands in the corner preparing the syringes. How Billy, sitting quietly on the tailgate of the pickup, looks like he might be remembering who he is and what it's like to smile.

I wonder if they see me, sitting on the cement rim of the stock tank, in shorts and sandals and with a clipboard on my lap. This is where I always sit, where I watch and keep the records with my pen. Straight columns, even and perfect. I am the record keeper.

"Leanne," Dad says. "This is X-1-5-1. Polled." He looks to see if I have heard over the din of bawling heifers, moaning bulls, barking dogs. I meet his blue eyes and nod.

"X151, polled," I breathe into my notebook, concentrating so that my writing is clear.

"What's 'polled' mean again?" Jess yells from where she's sitting on the fence.

"Means they were born without horns," Dad says as he sticks a needle in the cow's neck to vaccinate her. "It's good, because we're breeding it out."

"Why?"

"Well, would you rather be chased by a bull with horns, or without horns?"

"Oh."

"Bull," Dad says, scratching his head, concentrating. "But it's going to be a steer."

Under the category marked "Sex," I make a note of this.

"595 pounds." He squints at the numbers on the scale and then glances at me. "Got it all?"

I nod, then shift my weight on the stock tank and lean back on the wooden plank that runs down the middle. Closing my eyes, I turn my face toward the morning sun that's just risen above the top of the cottonwoods clustered around the house and barn, and the bright light pours down, seeping red through my eyelids. I dangle my left hand in the stock tank, swirling my fingers against the water. The warmth of sun and cold of water meet somewhere in my body and make me tingle all over.

Every year, the cycle starts here, with my hand in the water. After pregnancy-checking comes calving season, then we move the cattle to spring pastures, then haying, then weaning, then castrating, and then pregnancy-checking again. Some of the cattle are sent to slaughter, some we keep, some we sell. The records remind us, in case we forget, who mothered who, whose calf froze to death, which cows gave birth to twins.

Years layer up and weave together; bundles of images swirl together in my mind. I remember how turquoise the sky can be, how the cottonwoods drop golden leaves, how a calf being born slides from its mother and falls into a spring snow. From today I will remember Dad on the chestnut horse rounding up the calves, memorize Mom's slap on Billy's shoulder, capture Jess's singsong chatter to no one, absorb the heat and the sky and the smells. I will remember this warm fall day and the summer that came before and the winter that is about to come. Someday, when I leave here, I will close my eyes and remember, and I hope it will be enough to hold my heart together.

After the heifers have gone through, the older cows are chased in. Billy and Jack flap their arms at them until a few wander into the narrow alley that leads them to the chute. Jack sets an old manure-stained pole through the fence behind them so they can't back out, and then prods the first cow forward by twisting her tail over her back. She goes reluctantly into the squeeze chute, and Billy pulls the lever that catches her head in the metal bars. Behind her, the other cows stand, chewing their cud and blinking long eyelashes over deep brown eyes.

Just in time, Grandpa Ben's old blue pickup pulls into the driveway. He wanders up to us and hangs his arms over the top rail of the corral.

"Bunch of lousy-lookin' cows ya got here," he says to Dad but winks at me.

Dad smiles. "You just wish yours looked this good. Now get over here and help us."

Ben sighs and shrugs, and climbs over the corral fence. He wanders over to the box of shoulder-length latex gloves sitting on a rusted toolbox and pulls one on. Then he shuffles up to the rear of a cow and lifts her tail. "Ready," he says, and slips his hand up her rear end. The cow jerks and thrashes, but Ben's arm stays still. Silently, he feels around inside her. "Ninety days, I reckon," he says to me as he removes his gloved hand, now slick with slime and traces of blood.

I write this down under "Number of Days Pregnant," and shake my head in wonder. Ben is famous for his speed and accuracy. I wonder what he feels, how he feels, as his fingers glide around the very beginning of a baby.

"You want to give it a try?" he says, and when I glance up, I'm surprised to find he's looking at me.

Yes, I do. That's what I want to say, but the image of me in sandals, tank top, and glasses standing behind that great big cow makes me shy. I could do it, maybe, take the glasses from my face and rest my head against her. Slide my hand inside and feel the very thing that I'll name someday, some white-faced calf that's going to trot towards me, all curious, when I go for a walk alone out back. It will brace its front legs and stare at me, half scared, half playful, and I'll laugh and tell it about its mama and how I stood tiptoe and touched its unborn body, and how my family was working behind me, tossing complaints and laughter into the air, watching me all the while.

But before I can answer, Jack yells out, "Here comes Crooked Nose!"

"No, her name is Twisted Snout!" Jess sings out.

"X-4-2," Dad says, nodding at the cow's ear tag.

I duck my head, then look at Ben. He's still waiting for an answer. He's giving me a chance, I know, to join them. He thinks I'm lonely, left out. But what I'm hoping my crooked smile tells him is that maybe it's possible to love something the most from here, because from here I can see it all.

Maybe he knows. When he and my grandma Renny moved apart, he told me that it's somehow true that the thing you love the most can hurt your heart the worst. He said life is the fixation of points of interest and the flux of experience and what you come away with are the important stories and moments in your mind. He reckons that's how we survive the ache of it all.

I crinkle my nose at him and shake my head no. Then I turn to face the others and wave my arm toward them as if I am thrusting their comments away. "It is not Crooked Nose and it is not Twisted Snout. Her name is Pablo," I inform them. "Pablo Picasso."

This cow's nose was twisted when she was born and is curved slightly to one side. She looks crooked as she stands straight in the chute, blinking her eyes patiently as Dad rubs ointment on an area that looks like ringworm. She jerks her head only slightly when he clips the fly tag off her ear, and stands still while Ben feels inside her. She is one of the tamest, oldest cows of the bunch. I scan the corral until I find some of her calves, now grown and having calves of their own. There's

Soft Eyes, her first, and then Snot Nose, Crooked Hoof, Wild Mama.

When Dad opens the chute, Pablo Picasso doesn't even move. Dad has to pat her on the butt to get her to step out, and he laughs and reaches forward to scratch her ears as she meanders away.

"We'll sell Crooked-Pablo-Twirly-Nose after weaning," Dad says. Then, more quietly, "She's getting old."

I watch her go, thinking of how I'll have to put an "X" on her line, meaning she is no longer in the records. It's a little like what I thought at my Aunt Rachel's funeral—how hurtful it is that some of us are just absent, missing everything the future holds.

Dad and I take a break to irrigate the south pasture. It's late enough in the fall that we shouldn't even bother, but after the long summer of irrigating we can't seem to break the habit yet. I follow him out of the corral when he waves for me to join him. Even though we should hurry in order to get back and help, we wander slowly through the tall grass that spreads itself out below the blue mountains rising to the west. Dad walks with a shovel on his shoulder, I follow behind, and the dogs circle and play, pouncing on each other and rolling in the grass. The sun lights up the standing water in the fields, and the ditches sparkle as I hop over them, watching my dad watch his cattle.

The cows that have already been pregnancy-checked are out grazing now. Dad mumbles greetings or questions to each cow as we pass her. "Hey now, my big lady," he says to Big Mama, who always looks like she's pregnant, even when she's not. He nods at Elf Ears, who had her ears frozen as a calf, so they stayed stunted and small. He tisks and shakes his head at Sad Cow, who perpetually moos and blinks her mournful eyes. Perhaps this time she is missing her adopted calf of last year, who is being kept in a pen near the house. Her own calf died at birth, suffocated because the afterbirth wasn't licked off the face in time. I remember standing above a still body, steam rising from it into the cold spring air. Dad pulled out his large pocket knife, bent down, and began to cut away the hide from the still-warm body, pulling the skin from white flesh, miniature muscles. We put the hide over a shivering calf he got at the sale barn, then looped orange baling string under the calf's belly and tied it in a big orange knot on top. The calf looked so silly, like a present wrapped in death's skin—a gift for the mama cow. But Sad Cow kicked at it. The calf bawled softly and jogged to her bag of milk and Sad Cow backed away, kicking again. It ran to her once more, and she sniffed, her nose running over the dead calf's hide. The calf walked under her, buried his head into her chest, and moved down her side to her bag of milk. Sad Cow looked at us, my father and me, and then at the calf, and stood still as it put its mouth around her teat and sucked.

Dad looked down at me and winked, and I pulled out the notebook from my coat pocket and made a record, wondering at how this ordinary life is sometimes laced with miracles.

I wait until Dad moves the plastic dam farther down the ditch and shovels dirt on top to keep it in place. We watch as the water backs up and seeps into the field, curls through the grass, and spreads through the pasture. On the way back to the house and barn, I listen to him whistle, some slow tune that makes my chest swish open and my throat get tight. There will be times when I'll need to remember this day, I'd like to tell him. And when I do remember, I will have made time stand still.

I reach out and hold his hand. He looks down at me, surprised, and stops whistling long enough to smile, and then we walk on home, listening to his song, the drone of cows getting louder.

"Must be the bull I wanted run through," Dad says to me when we hear an animal thrashing in the chute. "Needs some shots."

"Vile Bull," I say.

He nods, agreeing. "Wild as sin."

As we turn the corner into the corral, I see the bull

blowing snot as he rages against the metal sidebars of the chute. His sides are heaving and his eyes are white-rimmed and wild.

Grandma Renny must have come while we were gone, because she's standing outside the chute now, egging the bull on. She's snorting and shaking her head each time it does, acting crazy enough to make us all laugh. Dad rolls his eyes and escorts her away and says it's time to get back down to business.

"Hey," Jack nods at me as I sit on the stock tank. "This is 5-3-1. Weight is 1,750."

I take my place to record the numbers. I'm still look-ing down when I hear Dad pull the bar that opens the chute. I expect to feel the rush of an animal going by, so I glance up in surprise at the silence. The bull has stepped out of the chute and stands next to it, then tosses his great head in the air. I see his sides inflate, the blow of snot from his nostrils. There is a moment of silence and stillness as we wait for the animal to move. I notice, in this brief moment, that the sun is being covered by an afternoon cloud, and in the shadow we form a tiny circle, composed of small specks. The bull, my dad and mother, grandparents, cousins, brother, and me, frozen for a second underneath a sudden dimness.

The bull turns, not toward the gate, but into the cor-ral where everyone is gathered. Though he moves away from me, I leap up and scramble over the closest fence at the same time I hear my father yell, "Whoa, everyone move!" I turn in time to see Jess crawl through the fence poles to the other side of the corral, Jack fling himself up onto a gate, Mom and Ben and Renny and Billy all throw themselves over the top pole of the fence. Dad turns toward me, the only direction he can, trying to gauge which way the bull is going to head so he can leap in the opposite direction, but it's too late and the bull gallops into him and sends him flying. He lands on his hands and knees and his feet scramble in the dirt to get him to a standing position. He does stand, just as the bull is about to charge him again. As the bull lowers his head and brings it up to catch and lift him, my father leaps forward toward the fence. The bull's head catches him, though, and my father's back arches backwards with the force of the blow, backwards as his body is thrown forward. His hands clasp the top fence rail and he pulls himself over. As he falls to the ground on the other side, the bull backs up and charges again. Wood splinters, buckles, but holds.

Already they are moving toward him, each member of my family rushing toward my father's body, and I whimper a prayer for him to move. He does then; he raises his head and pushes himself to his knees, and I am again aware of the dogs' barking, of Jack's whip cracking against the bull, of Jess's cries. The bull stands among these noises for a moment and snorts, tosses his head, turns, and calmly walks in my direction. He dips his nose in the stock tank and wanders past me, out of the corral.

I lean against the fence that separates us and watch him go, then press my forehead against the wood. It is warm from the sun and smells like it has been warmed and cooled and weathered for layers of years. I exhale into it, then climb down and walk to my father. The others are gathered around him and are asking if he's all right and he's ignoring them, intent on passing his hands across his body, feeling for hurt areas or broken bones. There is a cut in his thigh that shows through his torn jeans, which he examines and then shrugs at. He stands up straighter, then, puts his hands on his back, and declares himself fine.

Jack and Billy offer descriptions of the bull's charge and explanations for it. Jess runs to the house and returns with a popsicle for Dad at the same time Mom emerges from the barn with a dusty bottle of peroxide, which she pours over the wound, causing fizzing bubbles to drain bloody into the denim. He scowls at her command to go inside and soap up the area and change jeans. Everyone laughs, and it's over.

They disperse, at his command—Mom turns back to the syringes, Jess and Billy follow Jack, Ben and Renny go to round up a heifer. I stay, though, and watch him. He is looking at my notebook, which is lying in the dirt below the stock tank, the pages flipping in the light wind.

"Better get the records off the ground before they get stomped on," he says. When I don't move, he limps over to the notebook and bends, slowly, to pick it up. "One year I was going through the boxes at my folks' ranch," he says. "I found their records, which are just like ours—cow number, sire, year born, calves."

"Yes," I say, knowing this story. "Weaning weights, sex, cause of death."

"Except my folks also kept a daily record of everything. Prices of corn, wheat, what they got for each animal they sold. Year after year, column after column. Good things, bad things. Dust storms, how many hogs died of cholera, the year electricity went through. Then I came across this one entry. January second, 1959. 'Baby boy born,' it read. 'Twelve dollars to Dr. Blake.'"

"Seven pounds even," I finish for him.

"That's right," Dad agrees. "Seven pounds even."

I take the record book, which he is handing to me, and I look down at the last page, filled with my writing. As his kiss brushes the top of my head, I know there is no way this moment can escape the record in my mind. I will hold it there with the others. It will be a reminder of how a heart feels on a warm fall day when the cows are run through.

LAURA PRITCHETT grew up on a small ranch in northern Colorado. She earned her B.A. at Colorado State University and has done graduate work at Colorado State and Purdue University. After living in the Midwest for a number of years, she recently moved back to Colorado, where she lives with her husband and two children.

WINNERS OF THE MILKWEED NATIONAL FICTION PRIZE

To order books or for more information, contact Milkweed at (800) 520-6455 or visit our website (www.milkweed.org).

FALLING DARK
Tim Tharp
(1999)

TIVOLEM
Victor Rangel-Ribeiro
(1998)

THE TREE OF RED STARS
Tessa Bridal
(1997)

THE EMPRESS OF ONE
Faith Sullivan
(1996)

CONFIDENCE OF THE HEART
David Schweidel
(1995)

MONTANA 1948
Larry Watson
(1993)

LARABI'S OX
Tony Ardizzone
(1992)

AQUABOOGIE
Susan Straight
(1990)

BLUE TAXIS
Eileen Drew
(1989)

GANADO RED
Susan Lowell
(1988)

MORE FICTION FROM MILKWEED EDITIONS

AGASSIZ
Sandra Birdsell

MY LORD BAG OF RICE:
NEW AND SELECTED STORIES
Carol Bly

THE CLAY THAT BREATHES
Catherine Browder

A KEEPER OF SHEEP
William Carpenter

SEASONS OF SUN AND RAIN
Marjorie Dorner

WINTER ROADS, SUMMER FIELDS
Marjorie Dorner

TRIP SHEETS
Ellen Hawley

ALL AMERICAN DREAM DOLLS
David Haynes

LIVE AT FIVE
David Haynes

SOMEBODY ELSE'S MAMA
David Haynes

THE CHILDREN BOB MOSES LED
William Heath

PU-239 AND OTHER RUSSIAN FANTASIES
Ken Kalfus

THIRST
Ken Kalfus

PERSISTENT RUMOURS
Lee Langley

HUNTING DOWN HOME
Jean McNeil

Swimming in the Congo
Margaret Meyers

Tokens of Grace
Sheila O'Connor

The Boy Without a Flag
Abraham Rodriguez Jr.

An American Brat
Bapsi Sidhwa

Cracking India
Bapsi Sidhwa

The Crow Eaters
Bapsi Sidhwa

The Country I Come From
Maura Stanton

Traveling Light
Jim Stowell

The Promised Land
Ruhama Veltfort

Justice
Larry Watson

MILKWEED EDITIONS publishes with the intention of making a humane impact on society, in the belief that literature is a transformative art uniquely able to convey the essential experiences of the human heart and spirit. To that end, Milkweed publishes distinctive voices of literary merit in handsomely designed, visually dynamic books, exploring the ethical, cultural, and esthetic issues that free societies need continually to address. Milkweed Editions is a not-for-profit press.

Join Us

Milkweed publishes adult and children's fiction, poetry, and, in its World As Home program, literary nonfiction about the natural world. Milkweed also hosts two websites: www.milkweed.org, where readers can find in-depth information about Milkweed books, authors, and programs, and www.worldashome.org, which is your online resource of books, organizations, and writings that explore ethical, esthetic, and cultural dimensions of our relationship to the natural world.

Since its genesis as *Milkweed Chronicle* in 1979, Milkweed has helped hundreds of emerging writers reach their readers. Thanks to the generosity of foundations and of individuals like you, Milkweed Editions is able to continue its nonprofit mission of publishing books chosen on the basis of literary merit—of how they impact the human heart and spirit—rather than on how they impact the bottom line. That's a miracle that our readers have made possible.

In addition to purchasing Milkweed books, you can join the growing community of Milkweed supporters. Individual contributions of any amount are both meaningful and welcome. Contact us for a Milkweed catalog or log on to www.milkweed.org and click on "About Milkweed," then "Why Join Milkweed," to find out about our donor program, or simply call (800) 520-6455 and ask about becoming one of Milkweed's contributors. As a nonprofit press, Milkweed belongs to you, the community. Milkweed's board, its staff, and especially the authors whose careers you help launch thank you for reading our books and supporting our mission in any way you can.

Interior design by Dale Cooney.
Typeset in Granjon 12/16
by Stanton Publication Services.
Printed on acid-free 55# Frasier Miami Book Natural
Recycled paper by Friesen Corporation.